BECOMING COYOTE

BECOMING COYOTE

Wayne Ude

L^HP

$L^H P$

LYNX HOUSE PRESS
Box 800
Amherst, Massachusetts 01004

Publication of this book made possible in part
with support of the National Endowment for the Arts, a Federal agency,
and the Massachusetts Council on the Arts and Humanities,
a State agency whose funds are appropriated by the
Legislature and approved by the Governor.

Distributed by Small Press Distribution
1784 Shattuck Avenue, Berkeley, California 94709

Library of Congress Cataloging in Publication Data

Ude, Wayne, 1946-
Becoming Coyote.
1. Indians of North America – Fiction.

I. Title.
PS3571.D38B4   813'.54   80-27152
ISBN 0-89924-031-3 paper
ISBN 0-89924-023-2 cloth

Cover art "Becoming Coyote" by Abigail Rorer
Typography & design by Maggie & Christopher Howell
Manufactured in the United States of America
Third Printing, March 1990

BECOMING COYOTE

I

Mapping the Reservation

SOMETIMES EVERY NIGHT SOUND seems a beginning, and I lie in the dark straining for words spoken just beyond my hearing. By morning my neck and back are stiff; all day my vision blurs, my eyes try to pierce through to meaning. Sometimes the landscape wavers and shimmers — looking through bad glass or the heat waves over a highway in summer would be the same — and pain moves from my forehead backwards across my skull: then oblivion — no sight, no hearing, no sense of touch. Things exist still, but the connections are broken and I have no words, no meanings, I see no solid objects. Later — an hour, days — I feel sick, drunk-every-night-hung-over.

I listen to the old people. They say, in the old days men went out to fast, to seek out those voices just beyond hearing. Their vision would blur and they would pierce through to another world, come back with knowledge. I come back with a hang-over. And this: that some member of the Tribe is in trouble. So I get up, as soon as I can, head on down to the station, wait. If no call comes in, I spend a few unquiet nights. When I rest easily again, I know that whatever has happened is over, beyond my help. Later I may learn what it was; usually not.

I didn't sleep at all the night the Museum was robbed. Before sun-up I was at the station, waiting, but the call didn't come until the Museum staff went to work at eight. That it was only robbery came as a relief; I'd been certain someone was dead this time.

I did only a little cursing as I drove the quarter-mile from my office to the Museum. The Museum of Indian History the place is called — too grand a name for a one-story brick building, formerly Indian Affairs, with four exhibition rooms, a lobby, a couple of small offices in back. It's the only place we have for the old things. And breaking in there, destroying the exhibits, might not rank much lower in my book than murder after all.

I waited in the Museum's parking lot until the second patrol car pulled in. It's complicated for someone my size to get out of a car: shift the weight far back into the seat, open the door, work the legs out from under the steering wheel, use the open door to pull myself up. And as usual I managed to knock my hat loose. They don't make the doors large enough.

It was a bright, hot morning, not a tree for miles. I squinted across my car's hood at Jim Fisher and Eustace "Skunk" Bear, who'd gotten out of the other car and were waiting for me to tell them what to do. Some days it seems everyone on the whole Reservation waits for me to tell them what to do. I wiped out the sweatband before I put the hat back on. Keeping the sweatband clean is supposed to help your hair last longer. It doesn't, but I've got the habit now. Then I led the way into the Museum.

The staff wanted to tell us their theories about what had happened. I listened for only a couple of minutes before I chased them back into the offices to get ready for an inventory.

Then I put Fisher to work outside, checking the doors

and windows, and sent Skunk Bear with the fingerprint kit into the Hunting room, which had been hardest hit. If there was anything to be seen outside, Fisher would find it; he couldn't come up with a clear fingerprint if you made him one, but he could follow a trail almost like one of the old-timers. Skunk Bear, who couldn't track a moose across his own living room, was a little wizard with that fingerprint kit. Between them, they made one hell of a cop.

Once they were well at work I went into the room called "Plains Village Life," where the Tribe's Medicine Bundle was kept. It hung from the center pole in a model of an old-time Holy Man's tipi; one side of the tipi had been removed so visitors could see inside. I stepped over a barrier and went in for a better view of the Bundle. For several minutes I looked it over carefully — it hung slightly above me on the center pole — but I didn't attempt to touch it. That was reserved for the Keeper of the Medicine Bundle, and we had had no such person for a dozen years, ever since the last Keeper died and we hung the Bundle in the Museum.

The Bundle wasn't much to look at. Its outer covering was a rolled-up piece of animal hide, too old to identify, tied up with sinew. No one knew any longer what the objects sticking out from both ends meant, or even what they were, except that they were very important, very old, and very holy. The old people said other holy things were hidden inside.

They also say there used to be two Bundles, each with its own Keeper, but that fifty-some years ago an anthropologist persuaded an old and ill Keeper that his Bundle would be lost or destroyed if he tried to pass it on within the Tribe. And because the old man hadn't been able to find anyone willing to go through years of training to become Keeper of the Bundle, he believed the anthro and allowed him to take the holy Bundle away. They say — the old people do — that the holy man made that anthro promise that the Bundle would never be opened, and that he would keep it only until the Tribe was again ready for it. But the old man died without telling anyone the anthro's name, or even the name of his museum.

I think, sometimes, that one of these years I'll take a little time off, travel to the big museums back east, and that in one of them I'll find, hanging safely behind a glass wall, the Tribe's other Medicine Bundle. Once I've found it, I can go to law and recover it, then bring it back here to hang in our own Museum on the Reservation. Perhaps, after a time, someone will relearn the ceremonies for opening the Bundles, and they can again be active among the people. The trouble is, I'm no Holy Man, and I won't know the Bundle unless it's displayed with the Tribe's name. But we ought to have it back; the old people still insist that the Bundles are important — that we'll be only half here until we get the other one back — and they still talk of the missing Medicine Bundle, and of the Keeper who gave it away. One, Billy White Bull, doesn't talk much; instead smiles slyly, says he doesn't believe the Bundle is gone.

Skunk Bear came into "Plains Village Life" and started to work with the fingerprint kit, and I should have gone to look for the Museum staff. I needed to get them going on their inventory in the Hunting room now that Skunk was finished in there. But first I decided to take a look in that room for myself.

The Hunting room had been harder hit than had Plains Village Life. The thieves had gone through everything, and what they hadn't taken they'd left lying on display cases and even on the floor; the walls had been stripped bare. At first glance it was hard to tell if anything had actually been stolen; the room was a hopeless jumble of Indian hunting paraphernalia. It looked almost as though the Tribe, suddenly overtaken by "civilization," as they call it in the bars across the river, had stripped and left everything where it fell in their haste to escape.

I've been on the Museum's Board ever since it opened, but still I had never before seen the display cases open and

the old things out where they might actually be touched. No
one was around to watch as I took up an old bow that had
been left lying on one of the cases. I ran my fingers up and
down the sinew backing which had given the bow its strength.
The string was as old as the bow, but I could feel no give when
I wrapped an end around each hand and pulled. I strung the
bow, drew it to about half its power, held it there. Despite
the Museum's humidity control system, the wood had dried
and become brittle with age, and I could feel the potential
for breaking within it. Yet I could also feel that it had been
a strong bow, that it would still fire an arrow with force
enough to kill for those last few times before it would split
in my hands.

I put the bow back where I'd found it. Some of the
staff might come in, and it wouldn't do for them to find me
playing with the old things.

Nearby was a mounted figure which had represented an
Indian hunting buffalo from horseback. The figure was
naked, even its wig knocked to the floor by hands which had
stripped the clothing from it. The Museum staff had bothered
to stain only the visible parts of the mannikin — its arms, legs,
and head — before dressing it. The body was still yellowish-
white, making it look as though Indian limbs had been graft-
ed on. The horse and buffalo still appeared to be running
hard, but the half-Indian figure, looking scalped and despoiled
without its clothing or hair, sat uselessly atop the horse, its
arms in position to hold the missing bow, its glass eyes staring
into the buffalo's side as though sufficient by themselves to
bring the animal down.

I heard movement in the corridor outside. It was one of
the secretaries, a gray little woman who looked as though she
were afraid of a scolding for being there, or anywhere. She'd
come to tell me I had a telephone call, and could take it in
the office if I wished. I smiled, hoping the smile looked reassuring — she seemed to be a woman who would need a lot
of reassuring — and told her they could start their inventory

in the Hunting room. Then I went into the office to take the call.

It was my dispatcher on the line. Henry Elwood, who ranches along the highway east of the agency, had two horses missing from his home corral, and would I send someone out? Fisher had finished with the windows and scouted the parking lot as well as a parking lot could be scouted, so I sent him.

During the next hour Skunk Bear finished fingerprinting the Museum's rooms and also the window where Fisher said the thieves had entered. The Museum staff had nearly finished a preliminary inventory of the Hunting room, and the gray secretary was about to type a list of what was missing. It would give me something to go on until they could come up with a more complete list later.

I sent Skunk over to the station to start looking for a match on the fingerprints he'd collected — just one set, he said. As soon as that list was finished, I'd be heading back to the station myself. The whole thing looked like an amateur job — some kids or a couple of drunks. I leaned toward the drunks, myself, because they hadn't taken much, while kids would have taken more of everything than they could use. Drunks are fairly practical. While I waited, I wandered out to the parking lot to listen in on my radio. It was getting about time for Fisher to report, and I was thinking about calling him to ask what was going on at Elwood's. As I approached the car I could hear Fisher's voice, the tail end of something he was telling the dispatcher.

". . . Snook and tell him I've found something out here on Elwood's back road. Have him give me a call; I'll stick tight until he gets back to me."

I leaned into the car and picked my microphone up from the dash. "Mobile Two, this is Mobile One Jones. What have you got, Jim? Those horses?"

"Better than that, I think. I'm on Elwood's back road, about a quarter mile from the highway. I've got Charley Many Rivers' car, got two bundles of clothes in the front and

6

two of those old-time Indian saddles in the back. Some I.D. with the clothes — Charley and Joe Thunder Boy, looks like. No sign of them, but there are some tracks I haven't checked yet. Thought I'd better let you know first."

"I'll be there quick as I can, Jim. Base, did you copy?" The dispatcher came on. "Got it, chief."

"Tell Skunk to check Many Rivers' and Thunder Boy's prints against what we got in the Museum. Then have him get over to town and see what he can dig up about last night — who they were with, where they went, that sort of thing. And what they were talking about — see if it was a lot of this Red Power business. Send a truck out to Elwood's by the back way; we'll tow the car in, and Skunk can work it over for prints later. I'm on my way out to Elwood's."

I leaned on the horn until the secretary stuck her head out the Museum's rear door. I told her to send the list over when she'd finished with it, and asked her to call my office and let them know right away if any old-time saddles had been taken. She looked startled, and then she looked as though something had gone wrong and it might be her fault, but she was nodding as I drove off. I hoped it meant she understood.

I hadn't yet reached Elwood's back road when my dispatcher called: two old-time saddles, and two bridles as well, were among the items taken from the Museum. Elwood had two horses missing, and there were two piles of clothing in the car. It began to look as though instead of a minor crime wave I had either a costume party or an uprising. Probably those two war-whoops had gotten to talking Red Power with somebody, worked themselves up, and decided to go for a ride. They'd end up sleeping it off a few miles from the car, and later they'd come back, tails between their legs; still later they'd brag as though they'd actually done something. In the meantime, while they played Indian, I'd have to play policeman and try to catch them. And the whole thing wouldn't change anything for anybody anywhere.

Charley Many Rivers' old Ford sat by the side of the road

like a dead thing. In it were, as Fisher had said, two piles of clothing on the front seat and, on the back, two old-time Indian saddles that sure looked like Museum property. Fisher had already been through the clothes, and had found plenty of identification — driver's licenses, social security cards, even a checkbook belonging to Many Rivers, which surprised me a little: I didn't think any bank would have given him one.

I was glad to find out for sure that the burglary had been the work of a couple of drunks. It meant we didn't have to worry about the stuff being sold, unless they were planning to come back buck-naked from wherever they sold it.

Fisher and I began to work in a widening circle away from the car. In brush along the road we found horse sign — droppings, crushed grass, hoof-prints. The prints led toward the highway, which was just over a rise; while Fisher followed them, I climbed a small hill nearby and looked out over the countryside. I didn't think the horsemen would still be in sight, but I hoped to see something which might tell me why Many Rivers and Thunder Boy had come to this place to dress up like Indians and ride away.

It didn't make sense for them to have ridden either east or west along the highway in those outfits, and to the north lay the river, with no bridge for some miles in either direction. That left south.

From the hilltop I could see the prairie stretching south, gradually rising until forty miles off it gave way to foothills and finally to mountains along the Missouri. Here and there in the foreground were some cattle and a few horses, but nothing that looked like a man. Further off I could see only black dots on the landscape, too small to identify. Below me ran the highway; on it an occasional car or truck moved past. Fisher was working his way along the highway's far side.

I couldn't see anything out of the ordinary, and that bothered me. I had a feeling, similar to that sense of voices not quite audible with which I sometimes woke, that there should have been something unusual in the landscape spread out in front of me, and that the missing element was the key to what had happened the night before. But I couldn't quite remember what that missing element could be.

And I found myself envying those two ki-yis: riding for once in their lives like old-time Indians, leaving their cards and checkbooks and licenses behind, carrying instead the old bows and knives. I thought of the bow I'd handled back at the Museum, and of the windowless walls there, the hum of the humidity system as it filtered all odors out of the building. I wondered what the deerskin clothes would smell like as Charley and Joe rode south in the sun with the breeze in their faces. They must have been pretty drunk the night before, and by now they were probably sobering up, hung-over with the sun beating down on their bare heads. The ride would no longer be so pleasant as it had been.

Fisher was waiting for me at the bottom of the hill. He seemed puzzled. "I don't know about this thing, Snook. Found some prints all right, but I lost 'em about thirty feet the other side of the highway. Looks like they rode them two horses south all right, but there's some other tracks out there too, too big for a cow. Looks fresh, but I'm hanged if I can tell what it is. Want to take a look?"

We walked across the sun-baked asphalt toward the hard ground of the field. Fisher pointed out scuff marks and occasional dim horse-tracks as we went. When we reached a low damp spot on the far side of the barrowpit, he stopped and knelt by a larger set of tracks.

"If this is a deer, it's the biggest damn deer I ever heard of. Take a look here."

It was a split hoof of some kind, but, as Fisher said, too large for deer, and, judging from how deeply it had sunk into the ground, far too heavy. "Could an elk have wandered up here?"

Fisher shook his head. "Too big for that, even. Might

be some sort of clubfoot, I guess, some kind of cripple, but if it is, it's crippled on all four feet. There's just these few clear prints here. Everything else is cows or them two horses."

I started back to my car. "Well, maybe they saw whatever it was and decided to run it down. Must be some reason they'd stop right here after they left the Museum. I'll give Skunk a call on my way in and see how soon he'll have that tow truck out. You stay with the car until then, okay? Those two fellas just might come back when they get hot and tired enough."

I drove slowly back to the Museum, trying to think the whole thing through. It didn't quite come together: that Thunder Boy should get drunk, break into a Museum, and ride off dressed as an old-timer made as much sense as anything else he'd ever done, but why drive out to Elwood's place? And why Charley Many Rivers? Charley'd spent his whole life denying he was an Indian. He was carried on the Tribal rolls, all right — one quarter on his mother's side — and he was ready enough to sign up for commodity foods, government health, and a share of any money the Tribe squeezed out of Uncle, while he still insisted he wasn't Indian, but Metis — French-Indian mixed blood. Just like his grandfather.

I listen, when I'm not too busy chasing drunks, to the old people. They agree that old Bill Rivers, Charley's grandfather, got out of Canada just one jump ahead of the Mounties. But that's all they agree on — they can't even get together on what Rivers looked like.

The best story is told by Billy White Bull. Billy says that after the second Metis rebellion up in Canada — some time in the 1880s, that would have been — Rivers had to run south for his life because he hadn't just been in the rebellion, he'd led it; he was Louis Riel himself. Billy says the Canadians hanged a double, and knew it but hung him anyway to scare the Metis, and that Riel — Bill Rivers — got away. Billy has an old newspaper clipping he says proves it, a picture of Riel and his lieutenants.

10

Well, I've seen the clipping, and I'm not sure it proves anything. Rivers — I saw him once or twice when I was a kid — had been a long, lean man who looked as though the land where he lived refused to grow him proper food. And Riel, even in the picture Billy shows, was a short, squat, round-faced man. But Billy says that's what Rivers looked like when he first came over the line — that Rivers changed shape after he reached this reservation to escape from the Mounties who'd followed him. According to Billy, that shape-changing itself was proof that Rivers was Louis Riel and that the Canadians knew who'd died on their scaffold. Because why did the Mounties come after Rivers if he wasn't really Louis Riel? And if he wasn't Riel, they why did he bother to change his shape?

Billy always said Rivers/Riel wasn't only a Metis, but that he was actually touched with Coyote. Now by Coyote Billy didn't mean the little prairie wolf these ranchers waste their time trying to poison; he meant Old Man Coyote, Coyote of the legends, Coyote the shape-changer, the re-arranger, the crack-brain; the fellow who showed up after the earth was already here and fixed it up to suit himself. Billy always said that anything you couldn't understand about Rivers could be explained by his Coyote blood; and he said it would explain a lot about Charley, too, as soon as he got old enough to start shape-changing himself. Billy'd been telling me for the last couple of years that Charley was ready to start; he was past thirty, and the old-timers all say that's the age when a man changes from being a young man to simply being a man. They give their relatives that long to grow up; if they don't make it by thirty, no one expects them to make it at all.

Well, maybe Billy was right; maybe this museum break-in and costume party was just Charley's first stab at shape-changing. But that didn't help me much. I still had to figure out why he and Thunder Boy would drive out to Elwood's place.

That over-sized hoofprint might have had something to do with it; they'd taken mostly from the Hunting room, so maybe they'd seen something along the road, gone back to the Museum for equipment, and set out to run down whatever it was they'd seen. But what could that have been? Those two boys had both hunted deer and antelope hundreds of times, in and out of season. Even an elk up from the Breaks shouldn't have drawn them back a hundred years in pursuit. Now if there were buffalo around —

I almost drove off the road. Buffalo. Olaf Svenssen's place was just across the road from Elwood's, and Sven had just bought himself a buffalo. He'd had it for about a week. That was what I should have seen from the rise, and hadn't. Sven's buffalo. Those two crazy war-whoops had gotten dressed up and gone buffalo hunting.

I got on the radio. "Base, this is Mobile One, Jones."

"Base. What's up, Chief?"

"Listen, I want you to call Olaf Svenssen and see if he's seen that buffalo of his today. I think that's what Many Rivers and Thunder Boy are after, so if he hasn't seen it, tell him to get the hell out and look for it. And if Sven doesn't know where the damned thing is, I want you to call over to Chinook and get me an airplane as soon as possible. Got that?"

"Got it, Chief. Check on Sven's buffalo and get an airplane over here. Anything else?"

"No, that's it. Skunk get over to town yet?"

"Just left. Got a match on the fingerprints — Many Rivers, like you said."

"Figured. Thunder Boy was probably stealing Elwood's horses about the time Charley was in the Museum. After you get the plane, call Elwood and tell him Many Rivers and Thunder Boy are riding his horses after Sven's buffalo, and they're both dressed up like old-timers. That ought to make his day. Tell him I don't think they'll hurt his horses any, just tire 'em out pretty good. Be sure you get me that airplane, and rush that tow truck out Elwood's back road. I'll want Fisher to come along on the plane. That's all."

"Got it, Chief."

I stopped at the Museum just long enough to pick up the list the gray secretary had been typing. The staff had finished their inventory and were straightening up the place; they'd double-check as they went, but the inventory was pretty much complete. Outside of the Hunting room and a couple of things missing from Plains Village Life, nothing had been taken.

I took the list over to my office, a cubbyhole in the basement of an old house which holds all the Tribal offices. The walls are thin, and I could hear the dispatch radio from time to time as I sat at my desk. I haven't got any cells; prisoners we board in the jail of a small town just off the Reservation, where the local police are always happy to lock up a few more Indians.

The list contained about what I'd expected: clothing for two men, plus paint and a sacred pipe, and bows, arrows, quivers, finally saddles and bridles for two horses. The weapons bothered me just a little; my guess about the buffalo might turn out to be wrong, and those two ki-yis might be about to declare war on somebody. All I needed was a small Indian uprising on my hands.

The phone rang and my dispatcher answered it, then yelled through the wall that it was Svenssen; did I want to talk to him? I picked up the phone.

Now Olaf Svenssen's the only Indian with a Scandinavian accent I've ever known. His father had been white — Norwegian or one of those — and Sven had spent half his life trying to prove he was as Indian as the next fellow. His latest idea was to start his own buffalo herd; he'd bought that old bull, and now he was dickering for a couple of cows someplace over in Dakota. He'd talked of setting up a small shop to sell buffalo meat to the rest of the Tribe. He figured, or so he'd said in an interview in the Reservation's weekly newspaper, that buffalo meat was better than beef for an Indian. And while I kind of liked the idea, I wasn't certain just what I thought about buying buffalo over the counter in little cellophane-wrapped packages. Anyway, Sven wouldn't be too happy to hear my news.

"Sven. This is Snook. What'd you find out?"

"By golly, Snook, I tell you; we look all over, and we don't get a smell of that buffalo feller, and that's the trut'. Me and the boys, we find us a place where the fence is down and he can get out, but we don't find the buffalo. How come you thought he might be gone? Your dispatch' she don't say much, just that we should go look for him. You don't maybe arrest him for disturb' the peace, hah?"

"It's a long story, Sven, but I think a couple of the boys went native last night and are out chasing your buffalo. I'm going after them as soon as that Chinook plane gets here, and I'll let you know. In the meantime, you and your boys keep looking, okay?"

"Yeah, sure, we do that, only I don't think we're gonna find him, you know?"

"Well, let us know right away if you do, and I'll get back in touch the minute we learn anything, okay? See you later."

I could hear Fisher's voice over the radio in the next room. ". . . truck's here now, so I'm coming back in. That airplane come yet, or should I head for the office? Tell Snook I took another look at those tracks after I heard what he told you about it maybe being a buffalo. I dunno, I never saw a buffalo track, but it could be. Sure too big for anything else."

I stuck my head into the dispatch office. "Tell him I'm headed for the airstrip, and he might as well go over, too. And call Skunk and ask him to see if there's a book in the Town library that has a picture of buffalo tracks. Tell him to say it's for his kids or something, for Christ's sake. Fisher and I may be gone all afternoon, depending on how soon we find those fellas. You better call in White Robe and O'Day for back-up. I'll see you later."

I cursed and talked to myself some more as I drove to the airport. Many Rivers and Thunder Boy had gone buffalo hunting. And dressed like old-time Indians. And if I didn't stop them they'd kill the thing; those bows were good for a few shots yet, and that would be the end of Sven's buffalo herd. Maybe that didn't matter to anyone but Sven, but, dammit, I hadn't ever tasted buffalo either, and I'd only seen a few, over in a park in Dakota once, and it did seem a god-damned shame that an Indian, even just a three-quarter Indian, should go through his entire life without once tasting that meat.

In any case I'd have to go after them with the airplane, though I'd rather have been out there riding under the hot sun, even scorched and sunburned as they must have been, following that buffalo; and while they played Indian, I'd have to keep playing policeman, track them down, and stop whatever they'd set out to do.

The plane was circling for a landing as I drove up. Jim Fisher was already there, waiting for me. We'd have to fly over every inch of ground between the highway and the mountains, but our chances of spotting the hunters were good, if I'd figured things out right.

The airplane landed, and my radio crackled as I was about to get out of the car. I picked up the mike.

"Mobile One, Jones. What's up?"

"Base, Chief. Curator just checked those saddles in Many Rivers' car. Says they came from the Museum, all right."

A good sign. I relaxed a little. "Thanks. We're taking off now, but there's a pretty good chance we'll have to go after those fellas on horseback if they get far enough south. How about getting some gear together — sleeping bags, some extra clothes, food for a couple of days, and a pair of saddle horses. Get it all loaded and send O'Day about twenty miles south with it along the highway. It may turn out to be a waste of time, but I don't want to take the chance. We'll see you later." Without waiting for an acknowledgement, I replaced the mike, got out of the car, and walked over to the airplane.

I'm always a little surprised when one of Sam's old airplanes gets up in the air with my bulk inside. Perhaps it's the same surprise the old-timers felt when their visions worked and they, too, drifted above this same ground, saw it entire and at once, stood at the center of the universe and looked down. I can't see the land as they did; I know too much of boundaries, competing jurisdictions, treaties that revised borders always inward. Still, it's a satisfaction to look down and see the land as though it were whole, unlimited, free again.

We'd left the Agency behind and were flying east. Just to our north was the Grease River, and some forty miles further up was Canada. Those forty miles had once been part of what was then the Great Northern Indian Reservation, including everything north of the Missouri River from somewhere in the Dakotas all the way to what's now Glacier Park in the Rockies. Back then, the Agency had been right in the middle of our portion; now the Grease River was our northern border, and the Agency was up in our northwest corner. The Agency hadn't shifted; the Reservation had moved out from under.

Our plan was to fly over the spot where Charley and Joe had seen the buffalo, then continue on to the eastern border and criss-cross from east to west and back again, each time a little further south toward the mountains, until we'd covered the entire reservation. Three swipes, possibly four, would do it. The hunters might have hidden from searchers on the ground in any of the little brush-choked coulees running through the prairie, but two men on horseback — to say nothing of a buffalo — couldn't find much that would hide them from men in an airplane. If they made it as far south as the mountains, and especially if they got into the rough country south of the mountains, that would be another matter; but out on the flat they'd be easy to find.

Even at that, it was the third swipe, heading east again, before we saw them; and then it was the buffalo, not the riders, we spotted first. The bull was grazing in a little hollow on the prairie; we had to fly over a second time before we saw the horses, standing ground-tied about a mile away, and it took a third pass before we saw the hunters.

Charley Many Rivers and Joe Thunder Boy were creeping toward the buffalo, dressed in the old clothes from the museum, their faces painted beyond recognition. Their clothes, buckskin-colored and faded with the years, blended into the gray prairie so that, from a distance, it had been hard to see the men except when they moved. Their bows were out and ready, and only a small ridge remained between them and the buffalo.

Everything below me looked like a scene out of an old painting, and I felt for a moment as though I were powerless to alter it: the hunters, and the buffalo, too, could not see the airplane, or Fisher, Sam, and me in it.

Then the airplane's shadow fell across the hunters, and the one I thought was Thunder Boy glanced up. I relaxed, began to feel solidly in the world again. And yet not fully: Charley still didn't seem to know we were there, nor did the buffalo, which seemed also oblivious of the hunters as they crept toward it along the far side of that small ridge, stalking. I seemed to see three worlds at once, superimposed and shifting, as in the visions that accompanied my headaches just before blindness. Watching the two men below me as they stalked the old bull, I even thought I could see differences in the ways they moved, the ways they wore the museum clothing: Charley as though he had traveled entirely into the time perhaps a hundred years before when those clothes were new, and was now walking through that time toward the eternity within which buffalo had walked this continent; and Joe clumsily, as though he hadn't fully left his own time, hadn't moved completely into the world through which Charley pursued a still-older buffalo. Moving over the entire scene as we passed back and forth was the airplane's shadow.

Billy White Bull would have insisted that at least a part of Charley had always been in eternity, where the buffalo lived: that part from his Coyote heritage which was, if anything, older than the buffalo and its breed: existing before eternity, and surviving beyond it, Coyote, carrion-eater, hunter, thief, able to eat anything, whether alive, or dead, or rotten, or never alive, gathering everything to himself for no purpose but to keep his own shaggy, flea-bitten, crackbrained life going and turning everything to that purpose, just as Charley must be turning this buffalo hunt to some purpose of his own.

Just then the hunters topped the rise, and I yelled at Sam to dive at the buffalo, to frighten it into moving away before the men got within bow-shot. Sam, old cropsprayer, smiled with the pleasure of it and eased the plane over, brought it down to within twenty feet of the buffalo, then pulled up, motor roaring. My stomach was a bit queasy; the old bull ignored us.

We swung around and came back for another pass, closer this time: I could see grass moving in the wind created by the airplane's passing. The bull tossed its great head and switched its tail as though bothered by flies, then went back to its grazing. We dove on the animal twice more without results; the hunters were nearly within bowshot. Then Sam suggested that we try dropping something on the animal, try to spook it that way. He brought the plane over again, slowly this time, while Fisher and I slid back the windows on both sides of the cockpit and began dropping everything we could find: coins, chapstik, pens, pencils, jackknives out of our pockets, cartridges from our handguns, then our belts, shoes, even our shirts. The buffalo tossed its head and moved a few nervous steps.

As Sam came around for a final pass, Fisher and I combed the plane's small cabin for anything we could find: loose nuts and bolts, even a piece of panelling Fisher ripped off the walls, Sam's thermos bottle — first the coffee, then the cups, lining, and case — our sandwiches and the waxed paper they'd been wrapped in, and finally two rolls of toilet paper, one end of which we held so that the paper unrolled in the air. One strip draped itself across the buffalo's back, and the animal began to trot away, still not moving very fast. The hunters were running upright through the grass, all pretense of stalking abandoned, trying to get close enough for a shot before the bull fled. Sam told us to close the windows, then he dove the plane again, throttle wide open; I thought we came so close as to nearly graze the animal's back, was sure I could see the hair on its hump riffle in the prop wash as we passed. The bull began to run, heading south, away from the hunters. Sam came down at him again and again, and one of the hunters fired a futile arrow; I couldn't tell if the shot had been aimed at the buffalo or at us, but I was pretty sure Joe Thunder Boy and not Charley had fired it.

They had come further south than I'd expected, and it looked as though in a few hours they'd be off the Reservation. I had Sam try to turn the old bull east a couple of times, but it didn't work; we'd dive on it out of the southwest and he would turn away, but as soon as we passed he would wheel south again, heading for the river on the other side of the mountains. With the breeze out of the south, he could probably smell the water and the trees; that same breeze would keep him from scenting the hunters behind him.

A hundred years before, he'd have been on Reservation land all the way to the river, and there would have been no legal problem in going after him or the hunters; now the south slope and twenty miles of wilderness leading down to the big river belonged to the Bureau of Land Management. Those mountains had always been our center; summers were cooler there, winters milder, than further north on the prairie where there was no protection from sun or wind. Most of our people still lived in the mountains — on the north slope, at least — as far as they could get from the Agency and still be on the Reservation. No one had ever tried to live in the wild country to the south, which we call Coyote's Ground; off the Reservation, people call it the Breaks. Old stories claim that Coyote lives down there, and shakes things up from time to time, turning over in his sleep, or getting up in the night to piss. The old people say that accounts for the way the land keeps shifting.

Whatever the reason for it, the land between the mountains and the river does keep shifting and changing around — not in ways measurable on even the sensitive equipment at the college west of us, but shifts nonetheless; the outline of a hill or butte here, the path of a stream there, the shape of a coulee somewhere else, as though the land hasn't yet quite settled into any one pattern. The changes are just enough to keep any map from being accurate, and BLM has given up trying. Only an occasional hunter or fisherman, or a few cattlemen who lease the grazing, ever spend any time in Coyote's Ground, though there were gold mines for a while. But even the mines played out years before the geologists thought they would, and every so often one of the mining companies sends a new team out to see if they can find out what happened to the main vein.

It was only because of Bill Rivers, Charley's grandfather, that we didn't lose the north slope when we lost Coyote's Ground. That would have been sometime in the 1890's, when Rivers was middle-aged — I used to know the date, but it's forgotten now. He'd been living on the north slope for a while, but not even Billy White Bull is certain how long he'd been there before the Tribe realized that he'd established a small ranch on their land, within a few miles of where they usually camped in the winter. He seemed, like Coyote, to have come up out of the ground one day, or to have walked up out of nowhere and said, "This is my home; I've always lived here," not caring it was a lie, or changing it to truth as soon as he'd said it and wanted it believed.

Rivers' ranch ended at what became our south border.

Billy White Bull says Rivers put the ranch where he did because of his affinity with Coyote — that the Coyote blood
had drawn him when he came over the border from Canada.
When I asked why Rivers didn't just go all the way in and
settle in Coyote's Ground itself, Billy just laughed: no one
could live permanently in Coyote's Ground, not even his
relatives. The part of Rivers that had participated in the
Metis rebellions in Canada, the part Billy insisted was really
Louis Riel disguised, wanted permanence: wanted a one-
ranch Metis nation, as Billy would have it, a place he could
hold against whites and Indians both. Rivers knew, must
have known, that an Indian or part-Indian couldn't have
held land off the reservation in those days, and so he had to
choose land that would remain on the reservation. Coyote's
Ground wouldn't remain any one thing long enough even for
dreams of permanence. Just in the time Billy could remember it had been open land, reservation, gold fields, BLM
grazing, and now there was talk of a wildlife refuge.

   When the army came out of the fort which used to be
near our Agency and travelled down to the mountains for
what turned out to be our last treaty, Rivers somehow got
himself attached as interpreter. What lies, what dissembling
it took to manage that change, no one seems to know; but
he did it. Whether it would have worked had anyone but
drunken Tom Custer been in charge of the fort and the
treaty-making is another question.

   Custer had been assigned to the fort shortly after the
Little Big Horn, and had arrived accompanied by a surprising
number of whiskey cases, apparently ready to end his career
by drinking himself to death on the plains. He was no rela-
tion to George Armstrong Custer, but was known to his men
anyway as "Custer's Little Brother." He was under orders
from the army never to engage the Indians under any circum-
stances; the army felt it could not afford another debacle like
the Little Big Horn, especially not under the command of
another Custer. Tom Custer's men tended to agree.

He fought no battles against our people, rarely even sending out scouts; but from time to time — when drunk, or perhaps when suffering from an absence of drink; no one knows — Custer would appear on the fort's walls and direct his men to fire barrage after barrage of cannon fire into the empty prairie, cursing the savages he alone could see preparing to attack. The barrages were effective: they kept the Indians, and everyone else as well, miles away from the fort, since there was no telling when, day or night, the place might suddenly erupt. Perhaps it contributed to Custer's perfect record at retirement: no casualties, no defeats, no victories, and no engagements. Unfortunately for the length of that record, Custer's retirement came immediately after his failure to include the north slope of our mountains in the treaty which secured for the government the south slope and Coyote's Ground.

What happened at that treaty-making was fairly simple: when old Gray Elk, not a chief but appointed as a treaty-maker by the whites when they found he would accept bribes, agreed to sell all the mountains, Rivers translated a sudden stubbornness: the tribe would sell the south slope and Coyote's Ground, which no one could own anyway, but not the north slope. Instead, they would fight to the last man.

Gray Elk must have sat in astonishment as his easy compliances were met with surprise and then with anger from the whites. He agreed to more than the whites had asked for, offered them everything but the Grease River valley itself, but as Rivers translated the soldiers only looked angrier. And then, what must have completed his astonishment, came Rivers' translation of their reply: the whites no longer wanted so much land as they had told him before; they had asked that much only to test whether Gray Elk and his people were true friends of the whites, and they now sought only the south slope and the land down to the big river. Gray Elk must have been even further surprised when the whites said they would make no treaty that day, but would continue in the morning.

During the night the rumor spread among the tribe that Gray Elk had tried to sell the north slope, and that Rivers, speaking for him, had said no. By morning, Gray Elk had no choice but to say, in his own voice, everything Rivers had said for him the day before; and the new interpreter Custer had sent for overnight translated the words as Gray Elk spoke them. Custer agreed: his orders were to secure the gold lands at all costs, and so far no gold had been discovered on the north slope. None was ever discovered there; but that didn't save his career, such as it had been. After the signing, Custer retreated slowly toward the fort, stopping every few miles to send a few cannon shots along his back trail and into the empty prairie around. Again, he led his command to safety without casualties.

Behind him, other things were happening; Gray Elk was claiming credit for the treaty, saying he had met with Rivers secretly to arrange the trick they had played, and Bill Rivers was quietly riding back to his cabin with his bride, Gray Elk's oldest daughter. He had needed something more from that treaty-making than just a reservation border south of his ranch; he also needed a deed to that ranch, because his Indian blood came from Canada and had no rights on our reservation. In Gray Elk's daughter he had that deed.

Our airplane wasn't far from Rivers' ranch as we herded, or tried to herd, that buffalo. I wondered if Charley, who owned the ranch now if anybody did, might not head in there for the night, and I decided that that's where Fisher and I would camp. If Charley came that way, we might just get there ahead of him; and if he didn't but followed the buffalo into Coyote's Ground, Rivers' ranch would be as good a place as any from which to start our chase in the morning.

I told Sam to head back to the Agency, to be ready to get into the air at first light in the morning. Fisher and I would be on horses at the summit going down into Coyote's

Ground, and we wouldn't go in until we'd established visual and radio contact with Sam, assuming Charley didn't fall into our laps that night at Rivers' old ranch. There were spots in Coyote's Ground where radios wouldn't work — mineral deposits of some kind, I suppose — so we'd want to keep in sight of the airplane as much as possible.

We flew over the hunters on the way back. They were walking their horses, and both horses and men looked as though they'd gone about as far as they could that day. Maybe they wouldn't even try for Rivers' ranch; it was out of their direct line. In that case, they'd skirt the mountains to the west instead of going over the top. Either way, they'd have to cross the southern boundary we'd managed to hold since Rivers had first secured it for us, if they were to keep after the buffalo. And Fisher and I would follow.

II

A Peace Chief

WE CAME TO THE CABIN on Bill Rivers' ranch at dusk, Fisher
and I — with fresh shirts to replace those we'd dropped from
the airplane — in a patrol car driven by Skunk Bear, followed
by O'Day hauling two horses in a trailer behind his pickup.
I'd heard Rivers' cabin described by a man who'd seen it a
half-century ago, and it still looked the same: logs carved and
notched to fit at the corners, weathered and gray where their
color came through the dry gray mud which had spattered
shoulder high up the walls; only the shingles on the roof
were a darker color. The ground around the cabin was
packed hard, like the prairie north of these mountains,
though not cracked as the gray prairie itself would be this
late in summer.

The cabin's washed-out look should have made it seem
old and therefore permanent, something that, having lasted,
would continue to last; but instead the cabin seemed to be
turning into dust which would finally be covered by the grass
and brush which grew everywhere else in the valley. I knew
it could happen; there are cutbanks between here and the
Grease River to the north where the old-timers built stone

walls to funnel buffalo over the bluff's edge, and though it looks now as though only the bottom layer of stone is left to stretch back into the prairie, a little digging will show that it's really the top layer; wind-blown dirt has covered the rest, then built the prairie up so the surface is as flat and smooth as though it had been there forever. The dust could blow in around this cabin the same way, make it just another little green rise in the valley.

The man who'd first described the place to me had hoped every trace of Bill Rivers would disappear, as all traces of him must have already vanished in other places along his back trail. But that man was dead ten years ago, his ranch sold to strangers, and Rivers' cabin was still standing as solidly as ever, his fence lines clear if not unbroken. There was dust in plenty inside the cabin, though I knew Charley lived there at least part of each week. Much of the mess came from the sawdust and chips tossed out by Charley's sanding and carving. When I looked from the cabin's central room with its cookstove into the smaller of the two bedrooms Bill Rivers had added when his kids came along, I thought for a moment Charley had given life to a herd of miniature horses. He'd kept the best of his carvings and stored them in this little room, arranging them on the flat mattressless wooden bunks Rivers had nailed onto the walls.

While Skunk Bear made the place liveable with an old broom he found standing in a corner, O'Day and Fisher and I got the horses into the corral nearest the house, then moved Fisher's and my gear into the cabin. We put everything inside, even our saddles, bridles, and packs, to keep them away from the little leather-gnawers that come out of these hills after dark. Once that was done, we tested our portable radios once against the radio in Skunk's car, and then Skunk and O'Day headed back up the road.

Charley and Thunder Boy would be cold and hungry that night, sleeping on Coyote's Ground, perhaps huddled in their horse blankets if they could stand the smell of dried horse-sweat. They might even be too sun-burned to stand the touch of blankets or ground, might sleep sitting up beside the fire, if either knew a way to start one without matches. Certainly they'd sleep hungry; I doubted even Charley could hit anything with a bow and arrow. But he might come after the few blankets and cans of food he kept in the cabin. Fisher and I didn't want to show a light or chimney-smoke, so we ate a cold supper and planned to go to bed early.

Or rather Fisher planned to go to bed early. I decided to take a shift outside, up on the hill, to keep an eye open for the hunters if they did come sneaking out of Coyote's Ground. At best I'm restless, and this looked to be one of my bad nights, one when I'd just lie awake listening. This time, at least, I'd know what I was listening for.

Gray Elk's daughter didn't have a name after she married Rivers — if she did, no one ever heard it again, and it's forgotten now. Rivers' kids never heard him call her anything but woman, and she never spoke her own name. Billy White Bull thinks she was ashamed, but it has always seemed to me she must have hated Rivers once she knew she was only land title and incubator. I think she knew that someday the children would realize they didn't know even her name, and so would renew the hatred within which she raised them. She breathed hatred for Bill Rivers into the cabin's air, chinked the walls with hatred so that hating air could not escape, and in doing it she took back the heirs he'd gotten from her.

Rivers would have been too busy to notice, setting the ranch up the way he wanted it, on the old Metis pattern from Canada: not square as were American ranches, but longer by twice as much as it was wide, the long sides running uphill from the creek in the valley bottom, and the short boundary on the hilltop separating the ranch and reservation from Coyote's Ground to the south. Up there was where I wanted to be, where I could see the entire ranch and most of the valley, could perhaps even get behind Charley Many Rivers if he came over the hill and down through the ranch to the cabin.

And I wanted out of the cabin's close, musty air. So I got a jacket and a ground-cloth out of my pack and set out up the hill.

The creek bed behind me as I climbed was Rivers' other short boundary. Most ranchers would have tried to claim both sides of the creek and thus the entire valley, but Rivers hadn't. Perhaps he'd tired of empire-building in Canada — if he was Louis Riel — and this time wanted only enough for himself. Closest to the creek had been an irrigated garden, with the house and corrals a little farther back, and above the house an irrigated hayfield, with a dry pasture above that. One of his irrigation ditches had run along the fence between pasture and hayfield. It must have taken a lot of digging to build his ditches from further up the valley where the creek ran downhill out of Coyote's Ground and the land was too steep, the valley too narrow for ranching, but he'd done it. Maybe he'd thought he was going to live in peace with his neighbors, and later other ranchers would move in to help keep the ditch up — it was large enough to irrigate that whole side of the valley— but no one ever did.

From the hill-top I could see that the ditches were filling in and most of the railings had fallen from the fences, though the posts were still up. The gate Rivers had placed along the fence dividing his land from Coyote's Ground was gone completely.

Billy White Bull calls that gate the Coyote Gate. He claims it was there so Coyote would know that Rivers didn't intend to separate his place from Coyote's Ground. Billy says that Rivers didn't only mark his boundaries the way men do, with fences, but also the way Coyote does: by pissing on each post after he put it up, marking his boundaries with the urine scent. Only, Billy said, he didn't piss on the fence or the gate along the boundary with Coyote's Ground, because he didn't want to mark that off. And he didn't want the smell of his urine to invite Coyote to piss on the fence, because Coyote's piss burns right through everything but rock

— and it will burn rock, too, if Coyote pisses in one place often enough. Billy says that's one reason Coyote's Ground is so gullied — Coyote keeps pissing in there, burning the ground away as the piss flows down to the river. Billy says the Grand Canyon happened because Coyote settled in Arizona once and pissed in the Colorado River every day for about ten years.

I'd taken up my position outside the fence with my back against a lodgepole pine, so I could see the whole fence, see anyone climbing it or crawling through anywhere along the line — in fact, I was in Coyote's Ground. But thinking about Rivers pissing on his boundaries made me wish I'd smelled the tree trunk before I sat down and leaned against it, and I did go so far as to turn my head and take a deep breath over my shoulder — no piss smell, just pine bark.

Sitting up on that hillside in the dark, I felt almost like one of the old people waiting for a vision — but if that was true, and if the vision I was waiting for included Charley Many Rivers, and if Charley was Coyote, I was the only part-Indian in history dumb enough to go out looking for him. You didn't look for Coyote, the old-timers said; you avoided him if you could, took him as he came if you had to; but you didn't seek him. He was too irrational for that. He was powerful, all right — if he wanted a river somewhere, there would be a river there, though he was as likely as not to try to run the river uphill to see if it would work that way too, and then be swept away in the flood as the river came back downhill and cut its proper path across the prairie.

The man who'd first described Rivers' place to me had called that hill-top gate the Rustler's Gate. He claimed Rivers put it there so he could drive stolen cattle from the other side of the river across Coyote's Ground, up the far side of this hill, and over the crest into his own pasture. It was probably true; at any rate, everyone believes it. Certainly Rivers didn't bring any cattle with him from Canada when he came down, one jump ahead of the Mounties, and yet within three years he'd had a young bull and twenty head of breeding stock. People give him credit for not being greedy; he stopped rustling once he got his herd established, and let his holdings grow by less dangerous means.

But the ranchers south of the river had been hard hit by rustlers for several years, and they'd decided to do something about it. The Breaks — Coyote's Ground — were full of men who'd made a good living selling wood to steamboats on the Missouri until the railroads put them out of business, and some of those men had turned to rustling rather than move out when the bust came. In fact, the rustling was pretty well organized; the series of woodlots along the Missouri — and the Yellowstone — made good way-stations at which to hold rustled livestock, and pretty soon Montana cattle were show-ing up in the Dakotas, and Canadian cattle were coming down the Grease River to the Missouri, down the Missouri to the mouth of the Yellowstone, and then up the Yellowstone and over the hills into Wyoming. Dakota cattle were coming up the Missouri nearly to Fort Benton, and then north through Blackfoot country and across the Rockies into Idaho, and Idaho cattle were making the trip back. The same was true for horses. Rivers was never part of that; Billy White Bull says his Coyote blood made him too unpredictable to be part of anyone else's plans. But when a rancher named John McDonald got mad enough to go after the rustlers — and a lot of legitimate homesteaders, too, some people claim — Rivers just naturally got included.

MacDonald was the one who'd first described Rivers' place to me; he must have come over the hilltop out of Coyote's Ground about where I was sitting — MacDonald and a dozen men, looking forward to a quick judgment, a quick hanging. They'd made the same sort of trip a half-dozen times already that summer and fall, going after rustlers. Rivers had been left for last because they'd had to cross Coyote's Ground, the roughest part of the Breaks, to get at him. MacDonald said they'd stopped on the hilltop for a minute to look things over, and they'd seen Rivers working alone in his yard, pounding in a corral post as though expecting it to last forever, to never rot, break, or fall over, and so to hold permanently at least the corral ground. I had to admit that the corral was the only fence on the place still fit to hold stock without a lot of repair work.

MacDonald and some of his men had gone into Rivers' pasture through the Coyote Gate; the rest split up to ride downhill outside the boundaries, expecting Rivers to run, and not wanting to be trapped inside fences when the chase started. But Rivers had been waiting in the yard, no longer pounding fence-posts, merely leaning against the cabin wall near the only door, when MacDonald and his men pulled their horses up in front of the cabin. And when, at Rivers' suggestion, MacDonald looked back the way they'd come, he'd seen men in blue tunics, armed with rifles, stepping out from every little gully and piece of brush within gun-shot range — not just behind them, he'd seen as he turned back to face Rivers, but in a complete circle around the cabin and yard. All had been Indians; the uniform had not been Army, but Indian Police: blue tunics above buckskin trousers, moccasins on the feet, feathers in the hair, and rifles — not good rifles, not as good as the one that had been hanging in MacDonald's saddle holster, but good enough. MacDonald judged there were twenty of them.

Those days, the Indian Police were pretty much what MacDonald used to curse them for being: the Agent's private army, used to enforce whatever law he declared, whenever he felt like declaring it. The tribe didn't take them over for another thirty-some years. When MacDonald saw Indian Police aiming rifles at him, he figured the Agent couldn't be far off, and so he was expecting it when the cabin's door opened, and a small, greasy-looking man in a worn black suit stepped out.

MacDonald had known then he wasn't going to get his cattle back, but he decided to brazen it out as best he could.

He'd looked around slowly, made a show of counting the Indians, establishing in his mind where each one was, where each had been hidden earlier — the brush, the small draws around the cabin would have provided plenty of cover. He'd looked over his own men carefully, letting them see his deliberation, see that he wasn't being pushed or panicked into anything. Then he'd turned back to Rivers and the greasy little man standing next to him.

"You'd be the new Agent, then," he'd said, speaking to the little man, ignoring Rivers. "You think it's wise to be interfering in this?"

The greasy fellow'd made a slight bow, but it had been Rivers who'd answered. "You better come off that horse and step inside. I got something to show you in there. Besides him, I mean," pointing to the Agent. MacDonald hadn't moved, sitting the horse, looking at Rivers and wondering what he could have in that cabin that he could think might interest MacDonald. There'd been enough Police with rifles outside the cabin to hold his interest well enough as it was. "You better come on in. You still want to fight after, you can get back on that horse before the shooting starts."

Rivers had turned away from MacDonald, moved slowly, unhurriedly into the cabin, the Agent scurrying in front of him, getting out of his way. MacDonald had been left with nothing to do but get down and follow.

The first thing he'd seen inside the cabin had been Rivers' wife, lying on a bed over against the far wall. He'd stopped, stared at her, trying to figure why he should need to be shown this sick woman. Rivers' voice had called him away.

"She ain't it. Over here."

Rivers was standing by a make-shift desk, a sort of table with a crude set of pigeon-holes sitting loose on top. He'd handed a sheaf of papers to MacDonald, who'd started through them quickly, impatient for another look at the fixed hatred in the woman's stare at her husband. But then MacDonald had forgotten her, had gone through the papers a second time, slowly. They were Indian Bureau bills of sale, over a signature he figured to be the new Agent's, for cattle carrying MacDonald's brand. And he knew Rivers had him good, had him even beyond the twenty Indian Police outside, had him in law. Like every rancher along the river, MacDonald had sold cattle to the old Agent, and these bills of sale claimed that the new Agent had resold some of MacDonald's cattle to Rivers. Those cattle had been butchered and eaten some two years before, but there was no proving that.

A low moan, as through clenched teeth, drew his attention back to the sick woman. His eyes were used to the cabin's dim light, and he could see now that she was lying on her back, her knees up and apart, and that the sweat was running off her face, which was turned toward the three men. Her teeth were clenched, her eyes wide as she stared at Rivers. MacDonald also looked at Rivers, saw over his shoulder the Agent, the whites of his eyes clear, his face also shiny with sweat. Rivers looked disinterestedly toward the woman, back at MacDonald.

"Nothin' wrong with her. She's just birthin'. You read them papers careful?"

MacDonald didn't know how long he'd stood looking at Rivers before another clenched sound from the woman turned him out of the cabin, the papers behind him in a heap on the floor. He was on his horse, about to ride off, when Rivers and the Agent came out, with one more thing to say.

"Before you boys leave, you better take a look at my brand. Hate to have any quarrels over it later. You ride close by that corral on your way out, you can see it on them two horses. Here, I'll lead you. Hate to see you in such a hurry you miss it." Then Rivers had taken MacDonald's horse by the bridle, had led MacDonald past the corral, pausing for a moment to let him see the closest horse's near flank. The brand seemed to be a stick figure of a man; curious, MacDonald leaned forward, saw that while the figure had two arms and legs, it seemed also to have two trunks, and its head was split

into two half-moons, like a man divided, split in half — or like
the half-breed Rivers was. MacDonald cursed once, under his
breath, and spurred the horse away from Rivers and out of
the yard. One by one, his men followed, up the hill past
where I was sitting now, and down into Coyote's Ground.

I'd only bothered to look briefly into Coyote's Ground
before turning away. Down there things were so rough and
shadowed I didn't think I could see anyone coming anyway.
It seemed wisest just to keep an eye on the valley and along
the hill-top, try to spot Charley coming out — if he came out.
Billy would have told me that watching was useless, that once
in Coyote's Ground it was unlikely Charley would ever come
out again, unless as Coyote. On the other hand, if Billy was
right that Rivers' place had become part of Coyote's Ground,
I shouldn't be able to see Charley there, either. If he showed
up, I'd find out.

The child MacDonald just missed seeing born was to become one of Charley Many Rivers' aunts. His only uncle had
probably been tucked away in a corner somewhere. A second
aunt would be born some years later — the woman was, by
then, probably trying to keep any additional children from
Rivers; we knew how to do that sort of thing back then. And
finally, perhaps fifteen years after MacDonald's visit, Charley's
mother would be born.

The woman herself lived on for some years after the
third daughter came, but gave up no more children. Those
four — especially the boy — were enough to tantalize Rivers
with the prospect of passing on his little piece of Metis land.
And those four, the woman must have been finally certain,
hated him enough to destroy anything he passed on, if only
because it was his.

That was enough for her; she died then. The stories say
she died staring at Rivers with the same bitter hatred Mac-
Donald had remembered. Some claim she kept that look
until her relatives took the body from Rivers' cabin, and then
her face finally relaxed. One of the children, probably the

boy, had sent for the relatives; Rivers would have just tossed her in a hole somewhere, but he allowed the family to bury her properly, up in the hills on a scaffold.

No one can tell when Rivers realized that her death also took the children away from him, so permanently he could have no hope of getting them back. Perhaps he began to know when the boy slipped away to bring his mother's family to take her body. What he did about it wasn't clear right away, but before long he began to entertain young men travelling along the river, and after a while rumors began to float around. A little later one of them turned out true: the youngest daughter was pregnant. She was about sixteen by then, the most vulnerable of the children, maybe, the loneliest with her mother gone. However it happened, she gave birth to Charley Many Rivers.

Where that name came from no one knows. There is no Many Rivers family on this reservation, and no one here has heard of a Many Rivers anywhere else. People suspect it isn't a real name at all, but something Bill Rivers made up to get the child's birth registered. Some people say he chose the name because many rivers flowed into Charley's mother; others, because many people named Rivers were his parents.

Billy White Bull tells a story:

Coyote was married once, and maybe more than once. But his wife grew old, and his daughters were young. So Coyote went away for a time, and when he returned he no longer appeared like himself, but like a young person. He courted his daughters then, fooling them and his wife. And after a while he married the daughters, all three. Before long a child was born, with a long pointed nose, sharp ears, and paws where its hands and feet should have been. As soon as it opened its eyes, the child pointed to Coyote and said: "There he is! That is my father and grandfather!" The old woman peered closely at Coyote for a moment, then began to scold. "You shameless one, don't you know better than to come courting your own daughters!" And she chased him away. But that night Coyote crept back and changed places with the child, and was suckled at his daughter's breast, and grew up and became himself, Coyote.

Billy thinks that story told Rivers how to get away with it, since the boy was old enough then to have stopped him otherwise. The boy must have figured things out later, Billy says, because he disappeared not long after Charley was born. Billy figures Rivers — or Coyote — killed the boy. Others say that's right, but it was because Rivers found things were going on not only between young men visitors and the girls, and that's why he drove the girls out when the baby was old enough to be weaned and to toddle around a little.

One way or another, all four of Rivers' children left and Rivers kept the grandson, Charley Many Rivers, and a chance to hold the place after all.

But now the ditches were filling up, the poles falling from the fences; and though I'd seen all that restored, rebuilt, put to rights once before, I doubted the ditches would clear and the fences go up a third time. They'd been good fences; several years they'd stood after Rivers first put them up, though they began to sag after he died.

It was when the fences began to look pretty bad and the ditches to fill up that people figured out Rivers was dead. Charley hadn't told anybody about it — if it ever happened, if Rivers didn't just go off someplace — and since Rivers had quit inviting drifters in after the girls left, there weren't any visitors to find it out. Billy White Bull thinks maybe Rivers did just go off somewhere and forgot to come back — says that's the sort of thing Coyote was always doing, and maybe the Coyote part of Rivers just sort of forgot all about his big Metis plans and wandered off one day, got to following his nose and never came back. Billy says he'll wander by someday, and settle back into the old pattern for a while before he wanders off again.

Once in his wanderings Coyote became angry at the way he'd been treated by a village, and decided to take revenge.

36

He went up in the hills and found a cave, and he killed a deer
and made a beautiful white buckskin dress out of its hide;
then he talked a porcupine out of some quills, and he made
some dye, and dyed the quills, and decorated the dress and
some moccasins he'd made, too. He took hold of the hair on
his head and pulled it out long like a woman's, and he rubbed
musk on himself so he'd smell sweet and pretty. But his penis
kept rising when he'd look at himself in the water, he was so
pretty, and finally he took it and his testicles off and hid them
in the back of the cave, in a spring there so they'd stay good,
and he took the deer's liver and made a vulva to fasten on
where his penis had been. Then he headed down the mountainside to the camp where he'd been badly treated.

When he got there, all the young men were in love with
him, but the chief's son most of all. Coyote played hard to
get for a while, but finally he consented to marry, and so they
passed their wedding night. Coyote decided to spend the
winter there where it was warm and the chief's son would
provide food, and then in the spring he'd show who he was
and shame the chief's son and all the people forever.

But he was Coyote, and there was this little crack, maybe,
in his brain where his thoughts leaked out sometimes and kept
him from remembering things, and by spring he'd forgotten the
whole plan. He'd forgotten it so completely that in early fall
he bore the chief's son a fine healthy child, and each fall after
that he did the same, until there were three children living in
the lodge. Then one day after the third child had begun to
crawl around a little, the chief's son and Coyote were frolick-
ing in the lodge, the chief's son chasing Coyote around, when
Coyote made a long leap right over the fire, stretching his legs
out to keep from being burned, and the deer's liver vulva fell
off, right in the flames, where it shriveled and smoldered, giving
off a terrible stench. The chief's son stared for a moment,
saying, "But that's your — but that's — you must be Coyote!"
Then he raised a great cry of rage and shame, and all the
people came and chased Coyote far into the forest before he

finally escaped, with nothing but a thin dress, and winter coming on. Coyote had a hard time that winter, and it was long before he remembered exactly what he'd been doing in that camp, and where he'd left his penis and testicles.

The next time I saw Billy White Bull I'd have to ask him if he thought Rivers had wandered off somewhere and left his penis so he could get married. But Billy half believed Rivers had become Louis Riel again and gone back up to Canada to stir things up some more, and had left Charley down here on the ranch to provide him a refuge in case it didn't work out again. Billy figured that would make sense, because everyone knows things like that don't work until the fourth time they're tried, and the rebellions in the 1870's and the 1880's made two, and this time would only be the third. Though Coyote didn't think he was bound by that sort of thing, and so he was always messing up the rituals by doing them too few times, or too many, and then he'd get hurt. Maybe that had happened in Canada this third time, and he was still wandering around up there, trying to remember who he was.

Rivers' in-laws tried to take Charley home with them after people finally figured out that Rivers wasn't around any more, but Charley wasn't having any. Rivers had raised him to believe that he didn't have any relatives in this country, but just up in Canada — that he was a pure Metis, a full-blooded half-breed, if you will. Not half-French and half-Indian, which is where the Metis really came from, but some other being, grown up out of the ground itself, the color of the mud, or of the Grease River as it makes it mud-laden way downstream, and as much a part of the landscape as that mud. I'd heard there were other Metis who believed the same thing — that when the whites and Indians were busy fighting over the land, the first Metis just grew up out of the ground one day — first his head, then, by the end of the second day, his trunk; by the end of the third day, his legs; and by the end of the fourth day, his feet, and he walked off and started the

Metis nation.

So Charley kept fighting Rivers' in-laws every time they put a hand on him, and finally they left him alone on Rivers' place, though Rivers' kids didn't like that much. Rivers' kids — Charley's aunts and mother — would have liked to burn the place if they could have gotten it away from Charley. But they were still kin — and Rivers had a will on file at the Agency leaving the place to Charley. The in-laws let it be known that anyone who tried to run the kid off would have the whole clan on his hands.

Charley lived on the place without being bothered much by anybody. He had a gun and could shoot it, so he lived on venison or an occasional slaughtered calf and whatever he felt like planting in Rivers' garden. Occasionally the relatives would drop off some surplus food — flour, potatoes, some eggs if they could spare them. Charley was maybe fourteen; Rivers might have been gone as many as four years.

By then the fences were in pretty bad shape, and what was left of Rivers' cattle grazed all up and down the valley — no one else had ever moved in to neighbor Rivers — and even over the hill into Coyote's Ground. Then Charley started having trouble with John MacDonald, or rather MacDonald started having trouble with him.

After his visit to Bill Rivers, MacDonald hadn't crossed the river again for over thirty years, even after the government opened Coyote's Ground to fee-grazing and his neighbors started running cattle in the Breaks south of the reservation. Rivers hadn't stolen another cow all that time, so far as anyone knew, but MacDonald seemed to think that was only because swimming the stolen cattle across the river had gotten to be too much work as Rivers grew older; MacDonald wasn't about to swim cattle across the river himself and deliver them right up to Rivers' door. When word went around that Rivers was dead, MacDonald waited another two years to make certain before he began to lease ground on the reservation side, and to run a few head of cattle over there. When none of them disappeared — and MacDonald had men over there every week tallying — MacDonald stuck his neck out and moved enough cattle to really make rustling worth Rivers' while. No one bothered them either, and MacDonald relaxed. That was when the real trouble started.

Ever since anyone could remember there had been wild horses in the Breaks, and especially in Coyote's Ground, which is the roughest part, and so safest for horses, or anything else, for that matter. As more cattlemen moved in along the river, and as they started to run cattle on both sides, most of the mustangs moved into Coyote's Ground. By the time MacDonald's cattle came in, there was a pretty good-sized horse herd already there. Between the horses and MacDonald's cattle, the grass began to disappear pretty quickly. Back when the cattlemen had free graze, they didn't care how much the horses ate; but when the government began charging them so much an acre, they got a little tired of seeing horses eating up grass they were paying for. All up and down the river they began to slaughter mustangs. MacDonald and his men joined in.

Now Bill Rivers had had a small herd of horses — some he'd caught wild, some he'd probably stolen, especially early on when he was trying to upgrade his herd, and even a few he'd bought. When the fences he'd left behind began to fall, his horses joined the herds in the Breaks, and most of them probably ended up in Coyote's Ground.

Whether it was because he felt some of those horses were his, or Rivers had told him to keep an eye on Coyote's Ground, or there was some other reason, Charley Many Rivers, all fourteen or fifteen years of him, took the whole thing personal, and the next thing MacDonald's men knew, they had to stop and whip him every time they crossed the river to hunt down mustangs. Of course, Billy White Bull has an explanation for that, and it doesn't bother him a bit that it won't go along with his idea that Rivers went back to being Riel. Billy says that Rivers had gone into Coyote's Ground because the transformation had come on him; he'd joined his Coyote half and gone back to being Coyote again. Billy figured Rivers/Coyote was still down there, eating, sleeping, pissing, and trying to figure out what he'd been doing all those years he couldn't account for because he'd been Rivers/Riel and couldn't remember them very well. But Billy figures Rivers remembered one thing, all right, because not even Coyote could have forgotten it: that once before, when Coyote had first come to that ground, he'd been rambling through the hills, killing everything he met and leaving it where it dropped, until the earth itself stopped him: the ground opened up, or dropped away entirely; the trees sailed by his head, the hills stood up to fall on him. The river changed its course, and followed him, and he ran, and dodged, and ran again, and couldn't get away from the river — couldn't get out of Coyote's Ground; the hills rose up to hem him in. Coyote ran for days without sleeping, until finally he was squealing and begging and promising never to do that again, never to kill without need, and the earth grew calm and relented, and gave the ground to Coyote to live in so long as he kept his bargain. Billy figures Coyote remembered that, and somehow the Coyote part of Charley that Charley wasn't aware of yet remembered it, and out of terror at angering the earth again, breaking the old agreement, Charley's Coyote part pushed him to stop the slaughter. However it happened, Charley went after the riders MacDonald sent across the river to slaughter mustangs.

That was when I came into the whole business for the first time. Up to then I'd seen Rivers once, when I'd ridden into town in a wagon with my old man, and I'd never seen Charley at all. Rivers had been coming out of a store as we drove past, and I'd asked my dad who he was, because I'd never seen anyone like him; not only that he was lighter than most people on the reservation, without being nearly so light as a white man, but that he was dressed funny: home-made shirt and pants like everybody else, but with a wide sash around his waist, and a funny broad-brimmed hat on his head, the kind I later learned the Metis used to wear up in Canada. My dad said that was Bill Rivers, and I turned around to look at him until the old man made me quit staring, because even us kids had heard stories. As near as I can figure it, his wife was dead by then, the kids already off the place, and Charley must have been just able to walk, because later, when all the trouble started and Charley was about fourteen, I was in my twenties.

I'd gone to work for MacDonald the year he moved cattle into Coyote's Ground, and lucky to get the job. Most ranchers wouldn't have hired a kid from off the reservation, but by then MacDonald was having trouble keeping riders. And I wasn't a full blood; that time the quarter of white did me some good. It was my first paying job. Mostly I did chores and odd jobs around the ranch, but sometimes, if MacDonald was short-handed, I'd be sent out to help with the cattle. The other riders didn't care too much about having me along, but sometimes, after the trouble started, MacDonald used to talk to me in the evenings when no one else was around. He'd come out on the porch with a chair and a glass of whiskey and sit there and look off north, toward the river. From his place you couldn't see the river itself, but you could see the hills in Coyote's Ground leading down to where the river was, and with a good pair of field glasses you could sometimes see bunches of cattle and men in the hills. The horses didn't often come out of the trees then. MacDonald never did go over into Coyote's Ground, but he kept pretty close track of what went on over there. And if I was out in the yard, finishing up some job, or even just sitting in the shade, he'd start talking after a few drinks. Those were the times he told me about going over to hang Bill Rivers.

MacDonald never did send me over to work cattle on the reservation side; maybe he thought if I got that close I'd go home, or drive a few head over to somebody's place on the Reservation and divvy up, start my own herd the way Rivers had. But when his men had been fighting Charley for a few weeks, and some of them started talking about quitting if they had to whip that kid many more times, he got it in his head that I was a breed kid like Charley, and maybe I could do something about it. That's how I came to be riding alone in Coyote's Ground one day, pretending I was hunting horses, but really waiting for Charley to come piling out of the brush into me. That was Charley's only tactic; he didn't ever take a shot at anybody, but he'd lurk in the brush, and when he saw a bunch of cowboys shooting mustangs, or when he tracked them by the rifle shots, he'd come raging out of the brush into the closest man, usually knocking him off his horse if he was mounted, or knocking him down if he'd been firing from the ground, and then the two of them would roll around for a while until the cowboy came up on top and sat there punching Charley while someone brought his horse up. Then he'd give Charley a last punch, and jump off and run for the horse, and when he was up the whole bunch would head for the other end of Coyote's Ground. Since Charley didn't have a horse, they'd be free to hunt mustangs down there for a few hours before he could catch up to them again.

That was, like I said, the only time MacDonald ever sent me over to our side of the river. It was easy enough for the rest of MacDonald's cowboys to blaze away at those mustangs, but it would have been a good deal tougher for me. We like horses pretty well up here on the reservation; we'd spent generations walking from one place to another, and then the horses showed up from Europe, and for a hundred, maybe a hundred and fifty years, we had horses, and we were free like no people will ever be again. For a while, horses were almost like part of our bodies — we were almost one people, us and the horse. And even when I was a kid, just past twenty, I knew that the borders were tight around us, and it felt better to see the horses over-grazing the Breaks than it did to see cattle in there. I told myself I didn't have to actually shoot any horses; all I needed was to pull up near a small herd of mustangs, get off my horse real slow and easy, get the gun out, settle in to start shooting, and Charley would show up, sooner or later.

I'd about decided I was going to have to put a few bullets into the air to attract him, when he landed in the middle of my back. I was lucky; Charley always dove headfirst so he could start swinging his fists right away. If he'd come feet first, he'd probably have broken my back, and I'd still be out there, only by now I'd be bones, and those scattered.

Well, he landed on me and knocked me flat, and his fist came by and knocked my hat off, then the other one came by and took me alongside the ear, and about that time I let go of the rifle and started twisting around to try to get at him. I made the mistake of looking over my shoulder to see what he looked like, and a fist came by and got me on the nose. Then things were a little blurry for a while, what with my eyes watering, and I could understand why the cowhands didn't want to do this once a day for the next two years.

We threw up a good amount of dust; I'd get him by a leg, and he'd kick me with the other one, and I'd let go and grab an arm, and he'd whale me with the free one, and then I'd get him around the waist and he'd let me have it with both arms and both legs at once, until finally I got tired of it and popped him a couple, got him protecting himself, and then I threw him down in the dirt on his face, got his hands behind him, and sat down on his back where he couldn't reach me with his legs, or so I thought. He got a foot up there and raked it along my back anyway, but by then I had both his hands in one of mine, and when the foot came by again I grabbed it, too, tucked it in under my elbow, and took hold of the arms again, which were about ready to pull loose. Then I just held his face in the dirt for a while, letting him up every now and then to see if he wanted to talk yet.

"Talk!" he'd yell. "You Indian sonofabitch, I'll—" and I'd put him down in the dirt again, and after a bit I'd let his

44

head up to where he could spit dirt out without taking in a whole lot of new dirt, and ask him again if he wanted to talk, and he'd tell me I was a goddamned no good dirty horse-shooting bastard, and that he'd — go back down in the dirt again. I figured he'd get tired of it after a while, but he didn't; just kept cussing me. So finally I took my belt off and used it to tie his hands, then used my neckerchief to gag him, and carried him over to my horse where I could get at enough rope to tie him up right. Then I cleaned him up a little, brushed off what dust I could, and tried taking the gag out. But he started in again, so I just put it back, leaned him up against a log, and told him I was willing to wait all day until he was ready to listen a little and stop calling names. After a while he quit struggling. I asked him if he was ready to listen some, and he nodded. But he had more cussing to do when I took the gag out, so I just put it back in while I said what MacDonald had sent me there to say.

"Look, kid," I told him, "You're not saving those horses. You're just slowing MacDonald's cowboys up. You got to know that." He glared at me. "Now look, boy. MacDonald doesn't like having his men whip up on you every day, and he sent me to see if you and I can't work this thing out some-how. Now if you're willing to talk a little, we can see if we can't work something out, and I'll go back and try to talk MacDonald into whatever it is. You willing to talk now?" He nodded his head, so I took the gag out.

This time he wasn't cussing me, anyway: "Who the hell's this pissant MacDonald? What give him any right to shoot them horses?"

Well, that blew up MacDonald's theory that Bill Rivers' grandson had been lying low, waiting for him to push some cattle across the river, anyway.

So I told him who MacDonald was, told him MacDonald was leasing this land, and he laughed at that; said this land didn't belong to anybody, and MacDonald was a damned fool for thinking he had any rights over it. I tried to tell him the government owned the land, and it had given MacDonald rights on it, but he just laughed and said he knew about governments, that they just took land, didn't ever give it. Right there he was Rivers' grandson, anyway. Though he didn't seem to know exactly what a government was — almost as though it was some kind of monster from one of the old tales.

Well, I had a half-baked idea I'd been toying with while I rode over that day, and I decided to try it on him.

"Listen, Charley. You know and I know that MacDonald wants this grass for his cattle and he wants those horses off it." He couldn't argue that much, except to say, "Bastard's got no right," kind of low.

"Okay," I said. "Then is there any place we can run these horses off to?"

He actually thought for a minute before he shook his head.

"You sure?" I asked him. "No place up the river?" He thought, shook his head. "How about down the river?" Shook his head again. "All right," I said, taking a good breath, "what about away from the river?"

He looked at me like I was the dumbest thing he'd seen for a while, and he'd seen a lot of dumb things. "That's all Indian land. It's all fenced."

"Umm." I pretended to think for a minute. "What about that place of yours? Don't you have some land there?"

"Not enough," he said. "My fences are all down, and I ain't big enough to fix 'em. I couldn't put enough horses in there to do much good, anyway." He was starting to look pretty uncomfortable in those ropes, so I offered to let him loose and share a sandwich with him if he promised not to jump me again, or run off into the brush where I couldn't find him. "If you run off," I told him, "I'll just start shooting horses again until you come back after me. And next time I won't untie you at all."

When I mentioned shooting horses he started to get all

red-headed again, but then he sagged back down. The kid was starting to look beaten, and I might have kept at him until he gave up the whole thing.

But I'd gotten this idea in my head, and besides one of these days MacDonald probably would send me over to put away some horses myself, and I didn't like the notion much. The horses had been there a hell of a lot longer than MacDonald had, and I guess maybe I didn't like the thought that MacDonald should win this one completely. Maybe I'd heard too much about old Bill Rivers, and didn't want even Charley's little bit of him to lose to MacDonald, or anybody else. Or maybe I just went Indian for a little while.

Anyway, I took my time getting out the sandwiches, put on the pot for some coffee — had to send Charley into the brush for the water; I didn't know the country so well, and where the nearest creek might be was a mystery to me, but I figured Charley'd know, as much time as he'd spent skulking through this country chasing MacDonald's men around. "But come back, or I'll start shooting horses," I reminded him. He still didn't like that.

When he'd come back, and when he had himself a good mouthful of sandwich, I asked him how hard it would be to fix his fences if I could get MacDonald to send over a crew. By the time he'd swallowed and could talk a little, he was ready to tell me them fences wouldn't take much work, but there was no way in hell MacDonald would send a crew over.

"Well, he might, now. His men are talking about leaving him if he doesn't do something about you. How many horses that pasture of yours hold?"

"Not enough. Not by half."

I figured that was true. But I remembered something else MacDonald had told me about Rivers' valley. "Isn't anybody else living in that valley with you, is there? No other ranches?"

He shook his head, no, but he was puzzled. He didn't see where I was going yet.

"Anybody run cattle in there on the grass?"

No, nobody did that either.

I took another of those deep breaths. If I'd spent every day dealing with Charley, my chest would stick out as far now as my belly does.

"Well, kid, suppose I got MacDonald to fence that whole valley for you. Would that be enough room?"

Charley started laughing. "Nobody's gonna fence a whole valley! You been keepin' your head up your ass all week?" For a kid, he talked pretty rough, back then. Though you hear worse stuff from younger kids all the time now.

I let him laugh, then asked if the whole valley was unfenced; it seemed to me the other three sides would be fenced by the fellows who ranched on the far slopes of the hills, and only the south side would be open.

Well, yeah, that was right enough. I could see he was starting to consider it a little. "But how could we get them horses up there? Would this — what's his name?"

"MacDonald."

"Would this MacDonald send his men up to fence the whole place? That's a couple weeks' work, anyway. He wouldn't do that."

I didn't figure MacDonald would go for it either, but maybe, just maybe — he kept talking to me evenings about Bill Rivers, and I thought maybe this kid had MacDonald buffaloed but good. Billy White Bull told me, years later, that MacDonald had lived across the river from Coyote's Ground long enough to know that you can't fight Coyote, whatever his shape, and that he'd have to take any deal Charley offered him. I don't know; but something had the old man buffaloed. Anyway, we finished those sandwiches and we'd had some coffee, so I told Charley we'd better ride over and take a look at his home place, see if anything could be done. He got suspicious. "Why you want to see my place? What you really got on your mind?"

I told him MacDonald already knew where his home

place was, and if he wanted to scout it, he didn't need to ask Charley how to get there, and we packed things up. I got on the horse and pulled him up behind me.

We set out, him giving directions, because even if Mac-Donald knew where his place was, I didn't. My folks' place was up north, along the Grease River, and I hadn't been down south much. That was a long time before the new highway went through, and we just had wagons, anyway, most of us on the Reservation. As we went, I was checking out the ravines and gullies leading up from Coyote's Ground to the hilltop separating it from Rivers' place, because I had a notion about how to get those horses up the hill, too, if this whole deal would work.

There were some nice, wide gullies down in the Breaks, and they got nicely narrower and steeper as they went uphill. A fellow could drive a bunch of horses in at the bottom, put some brush-and-limb walls along the edges, and drive horses most of the way up the hill before he'd have to build regular fences. And even then, it would just be a matter of weaving poles through the brush to have a nice stock chute all the way up the mountain. That's how our people captured horses in the old days, and before that they'd done it to deer and antelope — and out on the prairie they'd used those rock walls to make the same kind of funnel for buffalo. I figured it could be done easily enough.

The valley was a perfect set-up for what I had in mind. The other three sides weren't completely fenced in, but they were close enough to it where other folks on the Reservation had gone to ranching, and Rivers' fence took up about a quarter of the open side. The plan would work, all right. Charley could see that, too, by the time we'd ridden all around the place. It was getting late by then, so I let him off back at the cabin, and told him not to go after any cowboys until he heard from me. He said he'd give me two days.

For a damn fourteen year old, without a solid fence or anything else solid on the place from the looks of it except maybe the cabin, he was pretty mouthy, and I almost told him so. But I had bigger problems. Like how to convince old John MacDonald he ought to put his crew to work for a few weeks fencing land for Bill Rivers' grandson, and then driving those horses into my ravine-and-brush stock chute up the mountainside.

I didn't even try to make it back to MacDonald's home place that night. Instead, I stopped down close to the river, and spent the night there in Coyote's Ground. I figured that if any tricky notions were apt to come to me, there wasn't a better place for it.

It didn't help me much, though, and when I came riding into MacDonald's place the next mid-morning, I didn't have any idea how to tell him about the notion I had. So I didn't try anything fancy; I just laid it out for him as though it was Charley's idea instead of mine, then sat back and waited. I'd made sure I was out of kicking range. We weren't in the house; he'd met me on the porch, stood for the first part of what I'd had to say, then sat down in his rocker. After I'd finished, he just looked at me for a while, then put his chin down on his chest and sat there, shaking his head.

"Now let me get this straight. You say the kid won't quit unless we leave the horses alone. And we can't do that. And so you say we ought to build a fence around the valley—"

"Not the whole valley. Just about a quarter of it. The rest has a fence already, Mr. MacDonald."

"Yes, All right. A fence around a quarter of the valley. And then we ought to build a stock chute—"

"I kind of thought the kid and I might be doing that while the fences go up. Keep him out of mischief, sort of."

"Yes. You did say that. Keep him out of mischief. I'm grateful. And so I should deliver sixty, seventy head of mustangs—"

"Excuse me again, sir. More like fifty, I think. We wouldn't have to catch them all, just enough to keep the boy happy. And then your men could take shots at the others, if they kept away from where Charley's like to be."

"Yes. Of course. If we're careful, we can shoot an occasional horse that's eating my graze. If we don't disturb the boy. And so I should deliver fifty head of horses to this Charley Many Rivers, and build him some good fences to keep them in. Did I ever tell you I went over there once before, to hang his grandfather?"

"Yes, sir, you have mentioned that."

"I thought I had. And so now I should do this."

"I'm sorry, sir. When the boy told me about the idea, I told him I didn't think you'd like it. But I don't know what to say, Mr. MacDonald. He's apt to keep after your men, and I don't think it would go over well if he got hurt. He's related to all those—"

"I know who he's related to. And I know he don't give a damn about them."

"No sir. But the word around the reservation is that they sort of keep an eye on him, because of his grandmother, you see. So it would probably cause some trouble."

MacDonald wasn't looking at me at all now, or talking to me, either. "I knew Rivers hadn't been dead long enough for me to run cattle north of the river. I knew it. I should just pull them cattle back out of there, but I can't afford to. I need the range. And every one of them cowboys will pull out on me if I do it . . . But if I don't every one of them will pull out anyway. And if that kid gets hurt, that family will get the Agent to raise hell until I lose that lease. The old bastard has me boxed again." Then he looked back at me. "You've got me boxed, you know that, don't you. You damned Indians always stick together. We'll do it. We'll have to. Next week we'll start in."

"Yes sir. The boy said he'd leave the men alone for two days, unless the building starts. Should I ride over and tell him it'll start next week?"

I could see the old man didn't like me much just then, and I figured I wouldn't be around the place too long after we'd got Charley's fences built. He kind of sighed, like he was finally giving up, once and for all. "All right then, we'll start day after tomorrow. I'll tell the men. You go over with them and get to work on that chute."

That was how Charley Many Rivers came to have his fences rebuilt the first time, and got a fence all along the south rim of his valley, and a herd of horses to go with it. MacDonald's cowboys bitched like hell about building that fence, and about chousing those horses into the ravine Charley and I tightened up. We'd had the easiest time of it, Charley and I, because we found the place Rivers had made into a chute to drive MacDonald's cattle, and we just rebuilt it instead of starting from scratch. The whole thing took about a month. And after it was all over, Charley just sat there, watching those horses. I don't think he ever tried to ride one the whole time he had them.

And I found myself pretty unpopular around MacDonald's place. He didn't talk to me in the evenings any more, and the men never had said much to me in the bunkhouse. So after a while I asked for a couple of days off to visit my folks, and I took out for the north end of the reservation, figuring that job wasn't worth coming back to, and not knowing where I was going to find another one.

I needn't have worried. While I was home, a fellow named Billy White Bull showed up one night. I knew about him — most people did. He was maybe fifty then, and he spoke for a bunch of the old folks who lived up in those same hills where Rivers' place was located. He wanted to talk to me, and I wondered about what; I'd never had much to do with those folks — my grandfather was a white fella, and I was a quarter white, and our family hadn't lived in any of the old ways since grandmother married out of the tribe. We'd been ranchers a long time before most others started doing it. So I couldn't figure what Billy White Bull wanted with me, or what the old folks could have to say to me.

Well, it turned out Billy wanted me to apply for a job.

The Tribe was taking the Indian Police away from the Agent; the Tribal Council was going to run it themselves, and they were advertising for three policemen and a chief of police. Billy wanted me to apply for one of the policemen jobs. I didn't much want to, mostly because I didn't think I'd get it, but Billy said I should. He said the old people liked me, because of what I'd been able to get John MacDonald to do for Charley Many Rivers. They said a man who could get a thing like that done ought to be one of the men who kept peace in the tribe, and that if I could settle that one, I could settle anything. He said the old folks thought I'd acted like one of the old-time peace chiefs. Personally, he thought I was just a lucky kid, but I should see how far my luck would last, and being a reservation cop would be a good way to find out — if I wasn't pretty lucky, I wouldn't last at all.

Every kid knows about the old-time Indian chiefs, and about what it was to be one, and what kind of man it took. You read about the war chiefs, but the peace chiefs, the men who kept things going most of the time, they had the toughest part. To have the old people compare me to one was more honor than anyone in our family had had since before Grandmother. But I still didn't think I'd get the job. Our family hadn't been popular ever since grandad, and my father hadn't helped any. He farmed pretty hard, and watched his profits pretty carefully, didn't spread the money around a whole lot. Billy more or less ordered me to try. He said I'd do better than I thought I would.

Well, I went on in and applied, and it seemed they were waiting for me. They knew who I was, and I filled out the forms, and a couple of days later, I was hired. Ten years later I was Chief of those same Indian Police that had surrounded MacDonald at Rivers' cabin; though none of those men were still on the Force.

That was my first run-in with Charley Many Rivers, and it turned out pretty good for both of us. The second time didn't turn out so good, a few years later; and now we were in for a third go-round, and this one didn't look like it was going to be even as good as the last one.

It wasn't getting any warmer on that hill-top, either, or any easier to keep awake, and after a while I didn't keep awake, I guess. When I woke up it was coming on to morning — you can feel the change in the air about the time the sun starts getting ready to come up — and so I stood, tried to stretch the stiffness out, and started down the hill to wake Fisher. By the time I reached the cabin, the east was getting a bit lighter, moving toward the false dawn, and things were becoming visible again.

III

In Coyote's Ground

FISHER AND I HAD ridden west, out of the mountains, to pick up the hunters' trail. These mountains are only a small outcropping along part of our south border, and the buffalo hadn't had to go through them; he'd kept to the high plains until they dropped away toward the Missouri, and then picked his way down into the wild country. The hunters' tracks followed. The buffalo had no trouble making his way down, but the horses slid some, and in that dry country the marks they left would show up for the rest of the summer. Next spring, run-off would leave a small cut and eventually a ragged slash down the slope. You can't do much in this country without marking the land, though sooner or later it covers your traces with scars that leave it only a little worse than before you came by.

Sam was already somewhere ahead in the airplane as Fisher and I led our horses down the slope into the rough country. Our radios were useless, full of static. But Sam had flown for us before, and we'd worked out some signals: if he found what we were after, he'd come back over, blink his running lights, and try to lead us; if he had nothing, he'd make two tight circles before he headed out again. For our part, we'd wave a shirt or jacket if we still had the trail, and if we'd lost it we'd wave our empty arms. For a change of direction — say we had to turn back for some reason, or the two hunters split up — we'd line our horses facing down our new path, or even one facing each path, and wait for Sam to acknowledge. Sam would wag his wings to show he'd seen us, and we'd be off again, hoping the radios would clear up. They never had, at least not this close to the mountains, though closer to the river we sometimes could hear him through the noise.

Whenever we track someone, Fisher scouts the trail and I follow along behind. That morning I was doing well just to keep Fisher in sight; I'd not slept much the past two nights, and my vision was blurred; the landscape wavered and shimmered. Billy White Bull would have told me I was seeing Coyote's Ground as it really is, and some of those mapmakers for the Bureau of Land Management might not have disagreed with him. But not even Coyote's Ground shifts as continuously as what I saw that morning, and I was afraid I knew what would come next: pain moving front to back across my skull as I lost my sight, hearing, sense of touch. Sometimes I can fight it off; if this time I couldn't, Fisher would have to leave me somewhere along the trail, come back for me when the whole thing was over.

Billy White Bull says there's a real world underlying this one, that ours is a shadow, a bad copy; he says the real world tries to force itself past my white parts into my mind. If I can ever learn to see that world, I won't have to live like a man without a vision any longer, can stop relying on dumb luck and Billy's good advice to keep me alive. Then, he says, I'll be able to deal on my own with Charley Many Rivers, with this Reservation, with myself. I didn't think Fisher would buy that explanation, and so I kept quiet, tried to fight off the dizziness, to keep from being left behind.

I said nothing when I saw one of the hunters riding back

along the trail toward us. Fisher didn't seem aware of him, though that may have been because the brush was thick and he was concentrating on the trail directly ahead: I thought again that this was going to be a bad day. Then Fisher looked up, brought his horse to a stop, and I felt better. When he spoke I felt better yet.

"Looks like our job's half over already. Unless there's two sets of lunatics running around down here." He started to reach for the rifle in his saddle holster, then didn't bother. The man approaching us didn't look dangerous. He swayed in the saddle, and as he came closer we could see blisters on his arms and neck where the sleeveless, collarless shirt — more vest than shirt — hadn't protected him. Indians sunburn, all right, though you have to know what to look for, and this would-be war-whoop was well done. All done up, too, from the look of him.

He'd come to within thirty feet, leaning and swaying forward over the horse's neck, letting the animal pick its way along, before he saw us. I'd figured it would be Joe Thunder Boy. He looked like hell. His face wasn't blistered as badly as his arms and neck — and even his chest where the vest didn't quite come together — but the paints had run as he'd sweat, and he looked more like a clown than a warrior. He raised one hand, called out: "Don't shoot, boys, I'm comin' in," sounding like an old-time hostile returning to the Agency after a few months of marauding the countryside, taking scalps and burning ranches. From where I sat, the only thing burned was him. The Museum gear still looked pretty good. He spoke again, from twenty feet: "Either of you boys got a spare shirt a man could keep the sun off with? Maybe a hat?"

Fisher was shaking his head and smiling. "Looks like we should have brought some sun-tan lotion. You're a real redskin now, Joe."

Thunder Boy tried to smile, but it didn't look like much. His lips were dry and cracked from the sun, and the smile started them bleeding a little. "The worst of it's my ankles, Jim. These pants don't quite come down to where the moccasins start — guess I should have stuck to my boots." His horse stopped on its own when he reached us. Joe had let the rein hang loose over the horse's neck; it must have been all he could do to stay on. "Don't suppose you've got a sandwich you don't need? This living off the land ain't what it's cracked up to be."

I didn't expect Charley, but I was watching the brush Thunder Boy'd ridden out of, just in case. Once or twice I thought I saw something move, but I wasn't trusting my eyes much. When nothing happened, I asked Thunder Boy.

"He ain't comin' out on his own, Snook. You'll have to chase him. I dunno; he's gone back to the blanket for sure."

"Well, let's get you fixed up, anyway." I passed over my canteen. "Take a little of this, and let's get down and see if we can do anything for those burns."

Thunder Boy climbed down from his horse and limped into the shade. Fisher came over with the first-aid kit, helped him take the vest off, then began salving the burns, shaking his head as he saw them up close. "These clothes look younger than you do today, Joe."

Thunder Boy was trying not to wince; Fisher's not the gentlest hand around. "I don't think these things are quite my style, Jim. Think I'll return 'em. Reckon the outfitter'll take 'em back, Snook?"

I'd pulled a spare shirt and pants out of my saddle bags. The shirt might ride loose enough on his shoulders, but I wasn't so sure about those ankles. I guess a man's ankles hardly see the sun from one year to the next if he's used to wearing boots, and it would be a while before Joe walked very far or even pulled on his boots.

"Fact of the matter is, Joe, you forgot to keep up the payments on those duds, and we're out here to repossess them, you might say." I dropped the clothes in a pile next to the discarded vest. "Try these; they're a little big, but that's probably what you need about now."

He looked relieved that we weren't hard-assing him, but he wasn't quite interested in the clothes yet. "What you reckon's going to happen, Snook?"

I sat down with my back against a tree, stretched a little. "Well, Joe, I'll tell you. Doesn't look to me like you did much but sweat into those clothes, and that's happened to them before. Since you came out on your own, I don't think there'll be a whole lot of trouble over this. I'd guess you can get off with a little probation, maybe a fine. You're not on probation for anything now, are you?"

"Haven't had any trouble since that fight about a year ago, Snook, and I've been clear on that for six months. Think they'll hold that fight against me?"

Fisher, who'd not only had to arrest Thunder Boy that time, but had to whip him on their way to the prowl car, was shaking his head slightly, and I was inclined to agree. "That was a whole different thing. And I imagine we'd both be willing to say you came out on your own and didn't give us any trouble. After all, you're armed and everything, could have just picked us off from ambush, counted coup and ridden home for a scalp dance. Main thing is to get everything back to the Museum. You didn't lose any of that stuff?"

The bow and quiver were lying next to the Museum vest on the grass between us. Thunder Boy glanced down at them and grimaced. "Hell, you'd be safer if I was shooting at you with that thing than if I wasn't. You ever tried one of those?" He paused. "Everything I had is right here, Snook. Even picked up that arrow I shot at your airplane yesterday — thought I might need it for that damned buffalo. There's only four arrows in that quiver, and I didn't think I could hit the sonofabitch more than once out of four. I think Charley's still got all his gear, too, but he's sure gonna take a shot at that bull."

Fisher had a layer of grease on Thunder Boy's upper body by then and was about to start on his ankles, but I wanted Joe out of those leggings first. My spare pants would hang on him, but they'd seen worse than a little grease, and there was no sense taking a chance with any of the Museum pieces. It didn't look to me like he'd want to let anything rub on those ankles, so I tossed a roll of gauze where Fisher could reach it.

I waited until Fisher'd finished before I handed Thunder Boy the sandwich I'd brought with the clothes. He went after it like he hadn't eaten for a week, but about half-way through everything came up again and he had to settle for water. It looked to me as though one of us was going to have to take him back; I doubted he'd make it very far on his own once the sun got hot. That was something I hadn't counted on, or I'd have brought along a third man. I'd have stuck with it if I'd been chasing a buffalo, and so I'd assumed both of them would. But I should have realized that Thunder Boy was likely to quit once he got cold at night, burnt on in the day, hungry all the time, and sober. I'd have to decide what to do now, but first I wanted to find out more about Charley. Joe could tell me that, all right, between pulls from my canteen, but as I listened, I wasn't really so sure I wanted to know. Thunder Boy's usually fairly quiet but this time the words came bursting out. The man had been scared badly.

"Snook, he's — he's one scary bastard is what he is. Last night I was ready to give it up, but he wouldn't talk about it. — wouldn't talk at all. He just sat there by that stinkin' little fire, noddin' and singin', with that stinkin' saddle blanket wrapped around him. It was like the damn fool didn't know he was hungry, didn't know he was tired, didn't know he'd been in the sun all day without anything to cover him. Just sat there, noddin' to himself, kind of singin'-like, and not talkin'. He was sittin' there last night when I fell asleep — if I fell asleep; maybe I just passed out. But he was the same way this morning, like he hadn't moved all night, kind of doin' that hey-hey-hey singin' like one of the old boys might, only you know Charley don't know any of them songs. The fire was down to ashes, and I didn't bother startin' it up again, because we didn't have anything to heat over it anyway, and it was gonna get hot soon enough. I was cold this morning, too, let me tell you. That old blanket ain't somethin' a fella can pull too tight around himself with this sunburn.- The old-timers must have been one tough bunch, that's all I can say. But when I got up, he got up, too, still without seemin' to see me, and then he put his blanket back on the horse and he got up on it, and by the time I was up on this one he'd started through the trees again, going on into the Breaks. I watched him for a couple of minutes, and then I decided I'd had enough of this shit — I've been Indian enough these last two days to last me the rest of my god-damned life. He didn't seem to notice I wasn't following him, and as soon as he was out of sight in the trees, I just turned around and took the trail back the way we'd come. I knew you'd be out after us pretty early, Snook, and I figured I'd just turn myself over. Didn't think I'd run into you this soon, though."

"You two ever get close to that buffalo again?"

"Hell, no, not after the way your airplane put the spook into him. You hadn't done that, I might have been back home by now, with some buffalo steaks fryin'. You sure played hell with that airplane. We could see that buffalo, all right, but we weren't gainin' anything on him at all, and when we got over the hill and into the rough stuff we had to slow down and watch his trail pretty careful so we didn't lose him. He don't leave much sign, really — not as much as you'd expect. A horse or a cow leaves a lot more. I s'pose he kept right on all night, or at least longer than we did, but we couldn't track him in the dark. Hell, I wasn't trackin' him any more by then, anyway, and I couldn't tell if Charley was, or if he's just gone crazy, riding around in circles not knowin' who he is or what he came for. Shit, when a man don't talk, how can you tell what he's doin'? . . . But we never saw that buffalo after we got in here last night. It got dark early on, really. Them horses was pretty tired, and I don't suppose we got here until late. Anyway, seemed to me like we ran out of light awful quick. I been riding back for a couple of hours now, so the camp is along here before too far. Ain't much of a camp — just the fire, and where I laid down, and where the horses were. But Fisher'll find it for you easy enough."

Fisher'd gone back to saying nothing, which was what he usually preferred anyway, but he looked over at me now with his eyebrows up and his head kind of inclined toward Thunder Boy. I nodded to let him know I'd caught his question.

"Yeah, Jim would find it easy enough. But it sounds like I wouldn't have much trouble, either. You don't look so good, Joe, and one of us ought to go back to Charley's place with you. I figure Jim could do that and still find me again, but I might not be able to find him if I went."

"That where you're workin' out of, Charley's? What you suppose he'll think of that?"

"Don't sound like he's thinkin' a whole lot at all right now. We ain't really workin' out of his place anyway — just stayed there last night, in case you fellas decided you wanted to sleep under a roof, maybe break open some of Charley's canned stuff."

Thunder Boy was a little more interested in that. "Canned stuff? You mean that sonofabitch has food back at that cabin and we been —? Well, he was too far gone to know he needed food, anyway. But I'd sure have liked to get at some."

"Old Sam's due over about any time now, Jim, so I think what we better do, first of all, is wait for him, let him know we've got Thunder Boy here and that you're taking him back. You should be able to use the radio again when you get up out of this stuff. Have Sam pass the word that Skunk should get out to Charley's place and bring a doctor with him. Might even want to get the ambulance, in case Joe's sicker than he looks. I'll keep on Charley's trail and you can probably catch up to me late today or in the morning. If I think I've lost him,

I'll camp right there and wait."

Fisher seemed to agree. We waited until we heard the airplane coming, and then Fisher and Thunder Boy got on their horses facing back the way we'd come, and I got on mine facing down the trail we'd been following. Sam circled twice to show he hadn't seen anything, then came over close to get a look at what was going on down where we were. I waved a jacket so he'd know I was still on the trail, but he had to come over a second time before he wagged his wings at us. Then he headed back over the Breaks. He'd come this way again about the time Fisher and Thunder Boy got to where the radio worked; Sam knows his business. The Bureau's always after me to put our airplane work out on bid, especially since Sam charges more than most, but I'm not about to do it, so we let Sam claim Indian blood and take advantage of Indian preference whenever the contract comes up for renewal. He's no more Indian than Leif Ericksen was, but he saves us money in the long run, even if he does tend to punch anybody who accuses him of being Indian — except right around contract time.

Fisher and Thunder Boy started back, and I moved on down the trail we'd been following. That damn fool Thunder Boy; he hadn't thought about the sun.

Coyote knows about the sun. Once he paid a visit to Sun's tipi, to see if it was as large and wonderful as rumor said. Sun invited him to come in, sit down, while he scared up some food. Coyote thought that would be good, but maybe instead of sitting down, he'd follow Sun and see how he hunted — because surely Sun would have some great power; what game could hide from Sun?

So Coyote crept along behind, watching. Sun carried a pair of leggings embroidered so they seemed on fire. Soon he came up to a clump of brush, and he stopped, laughing. "I know you're in there, you deer," he said, and he put on the leggings. Then he began to dance around the brush, and as he came around for the fourth time, he had his bow in hand, arrow ready. The brush burst into flame and deer came running out every which way; one ran right at Sun, who brought it down with a single arrow. Then he set to work to gut the animal, calling out, "Hey, you Coyote, quit hiding back there and come help carry your supper!" Coyote, looking a little ashamed — because while Coyote doesn't mind what he does, he does mind getting caught — came from behind a rock where he'd thought Sun could never see him. When the deer was empty, Coyote and Sun each picked up an end. "You see, this is how I hunt," Sun said.

That night, after they'd eaten and gone to bed, Coyote, who'd watched carefully to see where Sun hung those beautiful leggings, listened carefully to Sun's breathing. When Sun seemed asleep, Coyote crept over to where the leggings hung, took them down, and set off at a run. "Hoh!" he thought; "Now I'll be as great a hunter as Sun, and I'll never be hungry again — no more tricking Bear into bringing me food!"

He ran for what seemed hours, and then sat down to rest for a moment. But he fell asleep, and slept right through until he heard Sun's great voice saying, "Hoh! You Coyote! What are you doing with my leggings?" Coyote opened his eyes and saw that he was still in Sun's tipi, with Sun standing over him, and the leggings right there in Coyote's hand. "Oh, my friend," he said, "I took them down to look at them, and I must have fallen asleep while admiring them. They are such a wonderfully decorated pair of leggings."

Sun didn't say anything to that, but put the leggings back in their place on the wall. The next night Coyote tried again, after Sun was asleep. This time he decided to run all night, and to hide when it was almost time for the sunrise. He ran on and on, long after he thought he was too tired to run any longer, and when it came almost morning, he hid himself in a clump of brush and lay down to sleep. But he'd hardly closed his eyes when Sun's great voice woke him. "Hoh! Coyote! You've got the leggings again!"

Coyote opened his eyes, and he saw he was still in Sun's tipi, with the leggings tucked under his head this time. "Oh, my friend," he said, "you sleep well on this hard ground, but it hurts my head, and so I got myself something for a pillow during the night. I didn't know it was your beautiful leggings — they're much too nice to make a pillow of." Sun said nothing, but put the leggings back on the wall.

Coyote tried on the third night, this time hiding under some rocks when it came close to morning, and again the Sun found him, and again he hadn't left the Sun's tipi. The fourth night Coyote decided to just keep running into daylight, thinking that maybe something happened while he slept to bring him back, but this time when it got light he found himself running in the middle of Sun's tipi, halfway between the two walls. And this time Sun didn't take the leggings back, but said, "Coyote, I don't think you'll have any peace until I give you those leggings. But next time you think about taking something out of Sun's tipi, remember that you're always in Sun's tipi, which is the world. Now take your leggings and run along." And then Coyote couldn't see the tipi any more, but found himself out on the plains, carrying the leggings.

"Well," he said, "see what I've gotten this time by my cleverness," and he walked along, looking for brush that might have deer, or even a rabbit. After running all night he was terribly hungry. He should have been tired, too, but he was too excited to be tired.

Soon he came upon a little clump of brush, not too big, but he was too impatient to wait, and so he put the leggings on and began to dance around. As he came around for the fourth time, he had his bow out and an arrow ready, and the brush burst into flame, and a rabbit ran out, right past Coyote.

Only Coyote didn't shoot at it, because the leggings had burst into flame, too, and he was busy trying to slap the fire out. That didn't work, but just burnt his paws, and so he lay down and rolled, trying to smother the fire, but that didn't work either; instead it set the grass on fire. Then Coyote took off running for a river he remembered nearby, setting the whole prairie on fire as he went, and driving game of all sorts before him. If he'd stopped and shot them, he could have supplied himself with meat for a whole winter. But the flames were hurting too much, and he just kept running.

Finally he reached the river, and jumped in, and the flames went out; not even flames from Sun's leggings could burn up a river. But the leggings were ruined, and the fur on Coyote's hind legs was burnt off down to the skin, leaving him naked back there, and his front paws were burned too, from trying to slap the fire out, so that his fingers were all melted together and his hand didn't look like a hand anymore, and he lay in the shallows crying. Then he heard the Sun overhead, laughing at him for trying to wear his leggings, and since then Coyote hasn't liked the sun so well as he likes the moon. We know that because he never sings to the sun, but he likes to sing to the moon.

Coyote did get some good out of the leggings; later, when he could move around again, he went back through the fire ground and found many small animals which had been caught by the flames and cooked to a turn and he ate his fill at last — but his muzzle turned black from being thrust into the burnt bodies, and his coat has been spotted and streaked ever since from the ashes, and ever since he hasn't liked fire, or even bright light.

My eyes were a little better, maybe because of the rest, and I felt I could keep on at least as far as Charley's camp before I had to quit. Fisher would need at least four hours to get back to where I'd left him — longer if he had to wait at Charley's place for Skunk — and he'd still have to follow me a ways from there.

That might give me enough time; these attacks don't last too long when I lie down, let the thing take over completely. If I could find a nice, shady spot to curl up in, I might even be able to sleep through the worst of it — with a mild attack I can do that, sleep right through until the headache gets bad

66

enough to wake me up. The worst is over then, because I can't feel the headache until everything else has passed off, and I can see, hear, feel again. With any luck, I'd be back on my feet by the time Fisher caught up, and if I made it as far as Charley's camp, I could say I'd decided to wait there for my tracker. If I was real lucky and the attack passed off before Fisher showed, I could get back on the trail myself. In fact, I'd be able to follow Charley a little better then. This thing always leaves me sharp and clear; I never see so well, never hear so well, am never so aware as right after one of these things – even my senses of smell and taste are sharper. It almost makes the attack worthwhile.

And there was always a chance I would escape completely this time, could keep on Charley's trail without stopping. The trail was easy enough to follow; the buffalo seemed to have kept to one of the paths through the underbrush made by deer and cattle and even the wild horses which have come back into Coyote's Ground. All I had to do was watch for the occasional broken or bent branch left by Charley and Thunder Boy as they'd pushed through, check any prints I could see to make sure the horses who'd made them had been shod, and look as carefully as I still could at any side trails.

The horses running wild in Coyote's Ground were mostly descendents of those MacDonald's men had herded onto Charley's ranch, though some had drifted in from outside, and I suppose a few might even have been saddle stock that got loose. I doubted that any of Charley's original herd of mustangs were still alive down there; even the youngest would have been well over twenty years old, and that's pretty old for a wild horse, even one that's been cared for a little the first ten years of its life. And just as I'd been in on getting those horses onto Charley's place, I was in on getting them back into Coyote's Ground. At least this time it wasn't my idea, though some people give me credit for it.

After ten years Charley had three times the number of

horses we'd driven out of Coyote's Ground. Even that might not have been a problem, since the valley had good grass and water, and Bill Rivers had left a pretty fair hayfield for the winters. But Charley didn't ever sell a horse, or even break one to ride, and left to itself the herd kept getting larger. Sooner or later they'd have grazed that valley right down to the grassroots.

We were getting down to grassroots all over the Reservation just then. We like horses pretty well out here, and when people began farming and ranching their own land instead of leasing it out, they naturally started keeping horses. Some were working cow horses, but most were kept for the fun of it. A few people pretended they were breeding good stock — and a few were, even then, with blooded animals, papers, the whole bit — but most were raising pets, letting them have colts because watching colts was even more fun, and after all a family couldn't have too many horses.

Since almost everyone was doing the same thing, there was no market at all for horses around here, and even those who decided to sell off a few head couldn't get a decent price. Folks off the reservation knew they only had to go down to the bars when someone was winding down a week-long toot and offer a price that would buy the owner one more long night's carousing. We wound up supplying all the ranches around without breaking even on it. Really bad-tempered animals went to the rodeos, where they brought more money than any others we sold back then. Still no one much cared, so long as we had our horses. But Charley just sat on the steps of Rivers' cabin and watched his mustangs, and every now and then he'd walk out into the fields where they were, keeping his distance. His horses stayed a little bit wild, which was a good thing, as it turned out.

As time went on, the whole reservation became pretty badly over-grazed. People started having a little trouble with erosion — wind more than water, since we've got a lot of wind and damned little water up here — and the Bureau started issuing bulletins to warn people about it. No one paid any attention until some who'd moved on to their own places got tired of working and decided to lease again, only to find the leases paid less than before. Our pastures just weren't in very good shape.

The off-reservation ranchers pressured the Tribe, and the Bureau backed them up. To the Bureau, the whole thing looked like a nice little problem in range management, which is about the way the Bureau usually works: manage the land, let the people take care of themselves. Eventually the Council decided that something ought to be done; they passed a law saying you had to have so many acres per horse — not horses per acre, because our grass just isn't that thick. They made one rule, based on dry-land pasture, and then applied it to places like Charley's, where there was some irrigation, and where things are a lot greener than on the prairie. Of course they tinkered with the numbers every time a Council member got a new colt, but at least we had a rule, and it probably saved some ground.

Only they left it to me to enforce. The Bureau likes making rules for the Council to adopt, but doesn't care much for enforcing them. That's just too much work all the way around.

So I spent the next few weeks driving around the Reservation, telling people about the new rule, giving them a couple of months to get rid of their extra horses. I could only make about two stops a day, because I had the same argument every-place: hey, Snook, I know most of these people around here have too many horses, but look, I don't — this place isn't really over-grazed, it's just looking a little rough because of this dry weather; as soon as we get a little rain everything will be fine, you know that — hell, what would I want to keep so many horses for if they were gonna ruin my place?

The worst of it was, some of them were right; but I could only count the number of horses each family owned, divide that into the number of acres the Bureau said they had, and tell them to get rid of the extras. No matter how much I talked, I always fell back finally on the same formula: look, it's the law now, and I can't help it any. You've got to get rid of this many horses, or buy that much more land. The only way to change it is to go to the Council, and that's been tried. The next election is a year away, and you've got to get rid of this many horses in the next two months.

In the end, everyone went along, and I knew that even though I hadn't convinced anyone, they'd remember that I'd tried, had listened to them, when I could have just come in and said, first thing, look, don't give me any of that crap, get busy and get some of those horses out of here. When the old people get together, they'll talk for three days, until everyone's had his say again and again, and they'll try to get everyone to agree to what they're going to do. Sometimes it keeps them from doing anything at all, but Billy White Bull says that's better than making people angry. I can't go that far, but at least I can talk and listen for a while before I lay down the law.

Still, nothing could keep it from being a bad time. The market for horses disappeared, and people had to practically give them away. Even at that, a lot of horses went to the canners for dog food. That made people angriest, I think; no one said much, but at the next election, all the incumbent councilmen lost big. And the new Council didn't bring the law up for reconsideration; people knew it had, after all, been necessary — but that didn't keep them from taking their anger out by dumping the men who'd passed it.

I'd left Charley Many Rivers until last. I knew no amount of talking would convince him to sell a single horse, but I hoped that maybe, just this once, he'd see that he couldn't escape doing things the same way everyone else did them. I should have known better — hell, I did know better. I also knew he'd be impossible to deal with whenever I got around to it, and so it might as well be the last thing on my list.

But that had been eight or ten years before; I'd been

younger then, lighter on my feet before the weight came on, and I still hadn't managed to keep ahead of Charley that second time around: he hadn't been a scared, dirty kid anymore. Now, older, with these blind spells coming more often every year, I wasn't sure I was up to Charley anymore.

My horse seemed willing to amble down the path Charley and the buffalo had followed, so I let him have his head, only urging him on with my heels when he wanted to stop. The heat was coming up, and shadows crept into the edges of my vision, but I knew I could go on for a while. I tried to make myself watch the trail closely, but it was easier to slit my eyes against the glare, keep everything dim and so not see the darkness around my edges, let my mind wander.

When I finally came driving into Charley's yard, I found him sitting on the cabin steps, whittling aimlessly. That would have disturbed Billy White Bull no end; Billy would have been convinced Charley's Coyote part was getting ready to create something, and Billy wouldn't have wanted to be anywhere around. The last time Coyote got to whittling, he made the first human beings — on a dare, sort of.

Coyote was sitting around one day, carving aimlessly on a stick he'd found, and someone said there ought to be men in the world. Coyote didn't know what men were, but that didn't hinder his boasting; he claimed he'd already started carving some. The other one with him, who was Wolf, looked at the straight stick Coyote had been whittling, and laughed: men ought to have arms and legs, they shouldn't be straight up and down like a stake. Coyote said he was just adding those. Then Wolf pointed out that men ought to have heads, too, and Coyote was just carving that now. Wolf said one man wasn't enough, there ought to be more, and Coyote was just going for more sticks. He carved twenty like the first one, now that he knew what men ought to look like.

Then Wolf laughed some more and said men ought to be able to move around, and Coyote was just coming to that, and took the stick figures over and threw them into a hole he'd dug

out of an anthill the week before to see if the ants had anything good down there, and told the sticks to lie down for
a while and then become men. Coyote was tired of the whole
thing, and he figured Wolf would forget about the sticks down
in the anthole and quit bothering him about them.

The next day Coyote had forgotten the whole thing, but
Wolf hadn't, and made him come along to look even though
Coyote was busy and didn't really have time, and when they
looked in the anthole, the ants were swarming over the stick
figures, but the stick figures were just lying there. Coyote said
that's good, that's what I wanted, they're stubborn and don't
want to admit they're men, but after the ants bite them a
while they'll get up. They're alive now, they're just trying to
fool me by pretending not to be. He said that to Wolf, who
was laughing because the men hadn't come to life. Then the
two of them went someplace else for a while.

The second day Coyote wanted to go hunting, but Wolf
said let's go look in the hole first, so they came back. The
stick figures were still lying on the ground, but they were
quivering a little when the ants bit, and some of the bites
were turning dull pink in the pale wood. Coyote said, you
see, they're learning not to try to fool me. We'll look again
tomorrow. Wolf wasn't laughing quite so hard this time,
though he wondered if the sticks were really quivering, or
if the ants were moving them around.

The third day both of them wanted to go look. This
time there wasn't any doubt; the sticks were bouncing around
down there in the anthole, and turning bright red from all the
bites. Coyote nodded sagely as though this were just what he'd
expected, though really he was as surprised as Wolf, and said
they'd come back the next day. As they were leaving, Wolf
thought he heard a kind of whimper from down in the anthole,
but he didn't say anything.

On the fourth day Wolf wanted to go hunting, but Coyote
said no, let's go look at the people I made first, and so they
went and looked into the anthole. This time they saw some

fine, tall, strong people with black hair and eyes, looking up at them and dancing as they slapped at the ants, which were biting them unmercifully. "You up there," they called out. "Help us get out of this hole and away from these ants! They're eating us alive!"

Coyote looked over at Wolf and laughed. "You see how my magic works? They admit they're alive now! You in the hole! If I let you out, do you promise to stay alive, and to live here and be men?"

The people in the hole thought that was a strange thing to ask, since no one had told them this story yet and they couldn't remember ever being carved sticks that Coyote threw into the anthole, and so they said, "Certainly we'll remain alive if you let us out of this hole. If you don't let us out soon, these ants will eat us completely, and we won't be anywhere." Coyote said that might be a good thing, too, but he'd let them out of the hole anyway, and he turned around and hung his tail over the edge for them to grab onto. The people all grabbed hold and began trying to climb out at once, and Coyote, who'd forgotten that it hurts to have even one person pull your tail, was so startled that he jumped and pulled them all right out of the hole. He turned around and looked at all the men and women he'd pulled, and laughed again, and said to Wolf, "See, I pull them all out at once because I'm so strong. Your tail probably couldn't take that." Then he looked again and saw the women and said, "What's this? Oh, this is very nice, what I've created here!"

Wolf pointed out that his people were all red from the antbites, and Coyote said yes, that was part of his plan so you could tell they weren't wood anymore, and he told the people to go lie in the mud by the river until the ant bites were better, and he showed them where the river was, and what mud was. But even after the ant bites healed, the people didn't fade, but remained a beautiful deep coppery red color, and Coyote said, see, that's how you make people, though he was still trying to figure out how some of them got to be women. Wolf knew, but Wolf wouldn't tell him, and Coyote never did figure it out. Coyote's anthole was dug in the earth, of course, and earth is the mother, and she changed some of Coyote's figures into women, so there would be mothers and life could go on. Until then there weren't any women in the world, and since then there have been male and female in everything. But Coyote didn't really create women, and women have teased men ever since for being created by a crack-brain.

Billy White Bull would have thought of that story, and he'd have gone away until Charley was through whittling, and then come back. But it looked to me as though Charley was just slicing off some splinters for kindling, and I wasn't about to suggest he turn them into something else, so I got out of the car and walked over to sit beside him on the steps. He looked up at me, sort of nodded, but didn't say anything. I hadn't expected him to.

My horse stumbled, bringing me back to Coyote's Ground for a moment. The sun was getting high, beating into my face whenever I glanced up, and the shadows around my edges were growing. I could see Charley's face more clearly in my mind than I could the land around me.

He wasn't a whole lot to look at — hair a deep muddy brown with some red overtones, small narrow face, also muddy-looking, sharp nose that brought him to a point, though you couldn't call either his chin or his forehead receding — they just didn't stick out as far as that nose. Not a tall man, but with some muscle in his shoulders and arms, and the reputation of being a good worker, when he'd work. He'd done some sheepherding, had handled cattle a few times, but usually he hired on as a short termer when it was time to buck haybales, or bring in a herd, or brand, dehorn, and castrate young stuff. He could drive a tractor or a combine if you needed it — though he scythed his own hay by hand twice a year and stacked it loose, just as Rivers had done — and he didn't mind fencing, even if his own fences always looked ready to fall down before he'd fix them. A couple of times he'd gone out with fire crews in the summer, but he didn't seem to care for that.

He worked when he felt like it. He didn't need much money — only enough to keep his old Ford running and buy a night on the town from time to time. He didn't have any particular drinking buddies, but seemed to throw in with whoever was hanging around when he got to the bar. I didn't think anyone knew him well, or that he had any particular friends. There were still too many Bill Rivers stories being told, and too many people who weren't sure just who or what Charley might be, for anyone to get very close to him. At the same time, there was no reason not to drink with him. Besides, you never knew; if he did break loose, things might get kind of interesting, and you wouldn't want to miss it. People seemed to watch, even when they partied with him, and it set up a distance, an open space around him, that he probably wasn't even aware of, since it was so much less distance than Bill Rivers had carried everywhere.

It was that distance I'd been most aware of then, as I sat trying to figure out where to start. I'd put off even thinking about it, telling myself I'd have to see what kind of mood he was in, and go on from there. But he didn't seem to be in any kind of mood at all; he just whittled. People had been waiting to see what he'd do when it came his turn, and most of them hoped it would be entertaining enough to give them some fun out of that mess. I hoped it wouldn't be, and then again, I sort of hoped it would. Anyway, I was almost as curious as everyone else.

We sat for two or three minutes. Then Charley tossed the shavings and stick into the kindling box beside the step, turned to me, and said, "You gonna just tell me how many horses I got to get rid of, or you want to drink a cup of coffee first?" My face must have shown my surprise; Charley started laughing, putting his head down between his knees, then raising his face to look out over the valley, roaring out a high-pitched "Heh! Heh! Heh! Heh!" until I began to chuckle myself.

"I'll take the coffee," I told him when he slowed down enough to hear me, "If there isn't any poison in it."

He got up, smiling, and waved me toward the cabin door. "Hell, that wouldn't help me any. Have to poison the whole Council, and everybody'd know I did it even if I hadn't. Poison you and they'd send Fisher or somebody out, and he'd tell me the same thing you would, only he'd be meaner about it." I was just stepping into the cabin when he surprised me again. "Besides, as hard as you worked to get them horses up here, I guess I'm willing to listen to you tell me why they've got to go."

I'd always wondered if Charley realized I'd been the kid who'd helped him rebuild Rivers' chute up the hill. After I became a cop, I hadn't seen him again for three or four years, and I wasn't sure he'd recognized me then. He'd never said anything, even when I'd picked him up a couple of times for raising hell around town. I hadn't planned to mention it to him this time, either, even if he got difficult, but his remembering couldn't hurt. Maybe I could talk him into going along with things, and nothing much would happen. That would sure disappoint a lot of people. And maybe, I thought, riding into Coyote's Ground with my eyes giving out, all that would help when I caught up with him this time.

We'd sat at Charley's table and sipped coffee — hot, and strong enough to float a nail. One old boy I knew used to say coffee wasn't ready to drink until the nail dissolved in the steam before it ever hit the surface. He made his coffee in an old restaurant urn, one that didn't perk the grounds but just let them float around in the water while it boiled, with a screen at the bottom to keep grounds from running out the spigot. He cleaned it about once a year, and the rest of the time just added fresh water and grounds. Eventually he only had room in the pot for about two cups of water, and those sort of oozed through and out the bottom. Just smelling a cup of that stuff would keep you awake for a week. Charley's coffee wasn't that strong, but it would do.

I leaned back and looked around the cabin once before I started the bad news. All signs of Bill Rivers' family were gone — no cradles, no clothes, no woman's decorations hanging on the walls, nothing to suggest that the place had ever been lived in by anyone but Charley and old Bill Rivers. For that matter, Rivers was only present in that I knew he'd built the place, and that the little make-shift desk against one wall, for one, had been his doing. No blankets hung over the openings to the two rooms Rivers had added after his kids were born, though the nails for hanging them were still in place. I guessed Charley would hang blankets again come winter, cut down on drafts. The larger of those rooms, with the bed Rivers and his wife must have slept in, looked as though Charley were using it himself; the other, with four rough bunks tacked on the walls — flat wood platforms, with room on each for a single mattress, though there were no mattresses on them now — seemed to be his storeroom, the blanket removed from that door only so Charley could get a little cross-breeze through the rooms.

Charley was sipping his coffee, waiting for me to quit stalling, so I started in. "Well, I guess you've heard the worst of it already. I'll have to wander up the valley and take a count, then figure out how many horses the Bureau says you should have. Afraid I'll have to ask you to get rid of the rest — might be as many as half, though."

Light in that cabin was dim — it never had been wired for electricity, and daytimes only a little light came in the window and door in the main room where we sat. I was watching Charley's face pretty close, trying to judge his reaction, but I couldn't quite tell. He seemed maybe a little surprised — but most people were when we got down to numbers. Surprise wasn't it, though; maybe he'd just started thinking about this whole thing, and learning he'd have to give up that many horses was making him think harder yet. He took his time before he spoke, and then didn't sound as though his words were the same as his thoughts.

"Yeah, I figured I'd wait until I heard from you and found out how many. Guess I'll have a sale, same as every-body else, auction a few off. Can't see what—"

He broke off for a few seconds, then went on. "—what else a fella'd do. But first I guess you'd better give me a count, hey?"

I'd had as much coffee as I wanted on a hot day, so I pushed back my chair and stood. "Yeah, might as well get to it. Thanks for the cup — feels good to set a minute. Can I see the whole valley at once from the top?"

Charley was also on his feet, moving toward the door, leaving the cups sit. "You can see the west end from that gate up above, and then if you walk east a little, you can see the rest. Hill curves in just a little there, but once around the curve you won't have any trouble. I'll walk up as far as the gate with you — think I've got a piece of fence up there needs work."

I followed him up the hill, past the garden Rivers had laid out — there were some vegetables coming, a good stand of corn — and through a gate into Rivers' hayfield. The hay was coming along nicely toward a first cutting, and it looked as though Charley were keeping Rivers' ditches up pretty well. The fence didn't look as good as it might have; but I already suspected he waited to fix a fence until it was about to give in to the horses. Horses will rub up against a fence, partly to scratch themselves, and partly to see if there are any weak spots where they can get out. Then, half the time, they don't go any further than the other side of the fence, stop and graze there until you chase them inside again. They're like we are, sometimes: like to remind everyone they could run free if they really wanted to.

The gate coming out of the hayfield into the dry pasture above could have used a little work, but would hold a while yet. At least he was keeping the place up, not letting it go to hell the way he has since. The pasture was showing a little wear, I thought, and probably would show a lot more once his mares added another bunch of colts.

Charley didn't say much, just walked along, looking at what horses were out in the open. Most were up on the hillsides among the trees, or down in the draws where the taller brush might give them some shade, and we'd have to reach the hilltop before I'd see them. What brush there was in the pasture had never been very tall, and it looked as though the horses were chewing the leaves, killing it back still more. I was fairly quiet myself, dividing my attention among the place itself, the horses, and Charley. I didn't believe yet that he was going to take all this as calmly as he seemed to be doing.

The Coyote Gate still stood, Rivers' opening into Coyote's Ground, and now Charley's opening if he ever chose to use it. So far as I knew, he hadn't since we'd driven the horses through; when I walked over to take a look, I saw that the wire loops holding the gate closed had rusted and sunk into the post, coloring the wood around them. For a moment I leaned there, looking into Coyote's Ground at the top section of Rivers' chute out of the Breaks. Charley came over and stood with me.

I suspected he was thinking what I was, that it didn't seem worth it to save the horses from MacDonald's cowhands only to sell them off now. But I didn't believe he'd thought as far ahead as I had: that the only market for his animals would be the knacker, that we'd saved those horses so they could become dogfood. I wasn't about to speak it; he'd learn soon enough, and maybe by then he'd have lived with the loss too long to believe he could do anything about it.

"Well, Charley," I said, turning away from the gate, "at least we don't have to go down and fix that chute again."

He stood looking into Coyote's Ground and didn't hear me at first. When he finally spoke, his words again seemed not the same as his thoughts. "Guess that's pretty well grown over by now. Not enough horses down there to be worth it, anyway — and I don't guess we could get a crew for that kind of work nowadays." He grinned at me for a moment, and I grinned back, and then I sobered, thinking of MacDonald moving to the state capitol after he lost the ranch, becoming a kind of pioneer-in-residence at the Historical Society — a sort of pension for having been the one early cattleman who'd written his memoirs. He didn't mention Bill Rivers in them, as though he could pretend all trace of Rivers finally was wiped out by wiping him from one record, at least, of those years. And of course the Historical Society folks don't know any different. Now it was MacDonald of whom all trace was gone, his book long since out of print, his ranch sold two or three times since he'd lost it for debts and now broken up completely, parts of three or four other ranches. If there was a trace of MacDonald left, it was in Charley's horse herd and the fences his men had built. Those fences may not have looked too good, but they were standing — then, at least.

Now only Rivers' original fence around the cabin yard is unbroken; Charley's let the fence separating his land from Coyote's Ground fall apart, but the mustangs don't often come over the hill onto his place, and they don't stay when they do. Even Charley is too much human for them to be comfortable with. They'd gone completely wild again. I might have seen them at a distance there in Coyote's Ground, but I wasn't about to try to see anything at a distance; if I didn't try, I wouldn't have to admit how bad my eyes were getting. I was no longer tracking; probably the buffalo, and the therefore Charley, would keep following the path so long as it led more or less toward the river, and I would only have to worry about paths that branched off. Those, at least, I could still see.

Charley had wandered off along the fence, moving west from the Coyote Gate, and I started counting horses, taking the numbers down in my notebook. The trees and brush were thick with horses; Charley would have over a hundred, starting from the forty or so we'd run up the chute ten years before. His grass was pretty thin in the shade where the horses spent most of their time in the hot weather; it looked to me as though he'd have had to do something before long anyway, though, like everyone else, he'd have waited, left to himself, until it was too late, until the damage would need years to heal.

I walked along the crest and around the bend to where I could see the rest of the valley. There were almost as many horses in that end; Charley'd have had to sell off enough to flood the market all by himself, even if no one else had been selling horses. And those weren't very good stock; the mustangs we'd driven in had been scrubs, not good enough to tempt MacDonald's cowboys into roping them for saddle stock, and they'd already begun to show signs of in-breeding. On top of that, if what I heard was true — and I knew damn well it was — Charley hadn't broken any of them. Anyone coming to his sale could expect only a semi-wild runt mustang for his trouble. Gentled down, they might have made good kid horses, and the larger ones might have had stamina enough to be good, solid cow ponies — though they might not have had even stamina after ten years of easy living in Charley's valley.

I was admitting why I'd left Charley's place for last: everywhere else, I'd been telling people to live with their own mistakes, but here I was telling Charley to live with mine. If I'd left things alone, Charley'd have taken a few more beatings, eventually MacDonald's men would have killed most of those last forty, and the whole thing would have been forgotten, even by Charley. Instead, I'd managed only to save the horses from a quick death, with a slim chance to escape, for sure death in the boneyard and a lot more horses to die it. If Charley decided to fight, he'd be a lot tougher to handle than he was as a kid. If he forted up with his deer-poaching rifle, there'd be real problems. And I'd have to deal with them.

I wasn't feeling very happy as I walked back along the

crest and around the bend toward the Coyote Gate. Up ahead, Charley was crawling through the fence from the far side. For a moment he stood looking back the way he'd come, down past the chute, thoughtful as he had been in the cabin. Or, I told myself, as near as I could tell he was looking thoughtful; maybe I was just substituting my mood for his.

He turned as I approached. "Thought I heard something out there in the brush, but I couldn't find anything. What's the bad news?"

I shook my head. "My figures from the Bureau are down in the car — too bulky to carry around, and I'd hate to lose them someplace. Doesn't look real good, though. More of those animals than I'd expected — I make it a hundred and thirty some, though that's rough. Call it one thirty. Might be a little more than half will have to go."

He whistled softly, didn't speak as we made our way back through the pasture, the hayfield, past Rivers' garden to the house. Coming down through it like that, I thought the place probably didn't look much different than it had when Rivers was living on it, except that Charley'd torn down stretches of the east and west fences around the dry pasture so the horses could move back and forth along the crest. That old Metis rectangle was a good pattern for this country; I could see why they'd fought, declared themselves an independent nation, when the Canadians came into Red River and said they'd have to redraw the lines to square everything off. There'd have been room for two square ranches on each side of the river in that valley, with worthless patches of dry land left on the hilltops; but Rivers' way each side held room for three Metis rectangles stretching to the top, if anyone had been brave enough to live that close to Rivers. These days it would take the whole valley for one ranch to make a go of it. For all practical purposes, Charley owned the whole place, though technically all but Rivers' original piece still belonged to the Tribe, and the Council could have leased it if they'd wanted. They could now, as far as that goes. And I suppose if they ever got over worrying about Bill Rivers, they might.

Charley offered me another cup of coffee when we reached the cabin, but I turned it down. Walking that hill in the heat had warmed me enough already, and I didn't feel like sticking around while he thought over the bad news. I got my figures out of the car, checked how many horses he ought to have, subtracted that from the number he did have, while he sat on the steps, looking out at the valley.

"Well, Charley, it's rough. I'd say you should sell off about seventy-three horses — make that seventy, since I'm not sure of my count. Seventy, then. That's about as good as I can do."

I'd tossed my papers back in the car and was leaning on the fender, watching him watch the valley. He nodded, waited a few minutes before he spoke.

"Can't see any way of helping it, but I sure don't like it. Can I ask you a favor, Snook? Could you have some posters printed for me, maybe stick them up around the Agency or over in town? Just say an auction here in three weeks, on Sunday. Afternoon, probably. I'd rather not go around putting the posters up myself — you know how people talk around here. Could I get you to do that?"

I thought maybe I'd been listening too long to Billy White Bull and the old folks go on about Bill Rivers; I couldn't get used to the idea that Charley was just going to take it, hold a sale and give up the horses. Maybe I'd been wrong; maybe he'd kept those horses only because he couldn't figure out a way to get rid of them after he'd grown up and having them wasn't a kid's thing to do anymore. Maybe he'd only kept them because it was easier than doing anything else, or maybe he liked the way people walked soft around him because of all the old stories, and he figured getting rid of the horses would make him like everybody else, rob him of the knowledge that people were always sort of keeping an eye on him, waiting. But I couldn't blame him for not wanting to take care of the posters himself. Hell, he'd probably have drawn a crowd that would have followed him around as he tacked them up, egging him on to something. So I said I'd be glad to help him out. I'd have the printer send the bill — it wouldn't be much, anyway, for twenty or so posters. Maybe I could even get a couple put up as far away as Chinook or Malta, see if he couldn't pull some buyers from out of town.

I guess he'd known I'd say yes. Maybe he'd reminded me who'd brought the horses up here in the first place so I couldn't refuse to help get them out. But it wasn't much to ask, the way I was feeling. For a while we both looked up the valley, watching the few horses we could see from the yard, until I said I'd better be getting about my business. I told him I'd see him in a couple of weeks, that I'd probably come out for the sale and see how it went, and he nodded again, thanked me for taking care about the posters, and I drove away.

During the next three weeks I understood more completely why Charley hadn't wanted to handle the posters himself. From the time I went into the print shop to place Charley's order, I dealt with nothing but surprised stares, incredulous questions; and I seemed to have a few people with me all the time, asking what Charley had in mind. No one believed, any more than I had, that Charley Many Rivers was going to quietly sell off his horses. And certainly no one believed he'd sell to the dogmeat man, as we all knew he'd have to. The whole saga of Bill Rivers was dusted off and run by again; the old folks maintained that this was just what it would take to bring Rivers back from Canada, or up from Coyote's Ground, or out of wherever he'd wandered during the past twenty years. There were some new Bill Rivers stories, too, to account for those twenty years — one had him locked up in a Canadian jail the whole time, with the Mounties scared to death word would get out that Louis Riel had come back after fifty years and western Canada would secede again, until one night Rivers/Riel remembered who he was and changed shape, wriggled out under the cell door, crawled off, and a few days later remembered why he'd done it and changed back to Rivers. People looked strangers over carefully, wondering if they were Rivers in disguise. There were some new Coyote tales, too, and some old Coyote tales now had Bill Rivers as the hero.

I went back up in the mountains to talk the whole thing over with Billy White Bull. He warned me to watch myself pretty carefully, and not to trust Charley. The new tales, he said, were proof that Rivers and Coyote were still around somewhere, and that at least part of the time they were one shifting shape, because otherwise where would new tales come from? I made the mistake of suggesting that maybe the new tales were only stories people made up to pass the time, that they weren't based on anything that had really happened and so didn't prove anything. Billy's never looked at me like that before or since, and I don't much want him to — those black eyes narrowed as though wondering how someone stupid enough to ask such a question could possibly have lived long enough to get the chance. He wanted to know what kind of fool I thought would make up a Coyote tale; he said it was bad enough that people were telling Coyote tales in the summer, when they were apt to attract Coyote to listen — Coyote was always forgetting his own tales, and loved to hear them retold. In winter it was hard for him to travel, and so he might not actually arrive; but in summer a new tale Coyote had neither heard nor been in would surely bring him around, and if he hadn't done whatever was in the tale, he surely would as soon as he'd heard it spoken, and right there in your house, too. Then look at the trouble you'd have. Coyote tales are too dangerous, Billy maintained, even when they're true, to take chances with, and so new tales could only mean Coyote was still around. That's what they'd always meant, and things didn't change. New Bill Rivers tales meant he was still around somewhere, too. And Coyote tales being told about Bill Rivers simply meant everyone else had figured out what Billy'd known all along, what all the old people knew: Rivers was at least part Coyote, and therefore Charley was too. And I should be careful with Charley, or I'd find myself in a tale as well.

I figured all the talk would mean a good crowd for Charley's sale, if nothing else, though I doubted that many people would come to buy. It worried me a little — what if no one bid on a single horse, and Charley had the whole Reservation laughing at him? We might see something yet, and not very pleasant, either. I planned to be there myself, and I asked Fisher and Skunk Bear to show up as well — out of uniform, in their own cars, but with badges in their pockets and tear gas cartridges under the car seats where they could get at them quickly if I gave the word. I didn't think things would get that bad, but you never knew, with Charley.

I'd planned to show up at noon, when the auction was scheduled, but I was restless that morning, and it was only eleven when I drove into Charley's yard. I'd slept well the night before, which surprised me; it should have been another sleepless night, another warning.

A small crowd had already arrived — half-a-dozen pickups, four or five cars, parked in the yard. Probably fifty people were standing around drinking beer. I didn't care for that this early — put booze together with what was going to happen to Charley's horses, and we could have real trouble. Bothering me more was the state of Charley's corrals: they were empty. I didn't think he could sell animals right out of the field — people always want to see what they're being asked to bid on. Maybe he'd realized that there was no market left, or maybe he'd figured out that only the knacker would be bidding, and he planned to let the buyers round up their own horses, so that at least he wouldn't have to help put them on the road to dogmeat.

The crowd seemed in a good mood, though of course the beer would help. People stood in small groups, talking and laughing, more noisy than I'd expected this early. They should have been quieter, more watchful, making sure they didn't miss anything.

Charley's liquor permit had come through my office after the Council voted to grant it, so I'd known he'd have beer for sale. We usually allow beer as part of an auction; it tends to help draw a crowd, and sometimes, if enough beer gets drunk, it helps the prices. But I wasn't prepared for what I saw through the open door of Charley's cabin: stack after stack of beer cases, with ice blocks between, so the whole main room was a beer ice-house. It looked as though the horses might be just an added attraction for the beer business. Maybe Charley had some idea about selling enough beer to pay for shipping the horses somewhere, or even buying more land so he could keep the whole herd.

One of his drinking buddies was selling beer through the cabin's front window, and Charley didn't have much to do but sit on the steps and watch the crowd. He wasn't watching horses up the valley, because there weren't any in sight. I nodded to him, but that was all; I wanted to look around a little before I went up against him, if I had to.

About that time Fisher showed. He was a little early, too, but that was just as well, since I needed somebody to keep an eye on things down below while I went up the hill to see where the horses were. Fisher was looking at the beer like a thirsty man, so I suggested he go light on the stuff until we had some idea what was going on.

Then I started uphill, walking slowly in the heat, looking things over as carefully as I could. Charley'd fixed Rivers' original fences so it would be possible to hold stock on his own land instead of letting them run through the valley. That would have been a good sign, if there'd been any horses inside those fences, but there weren't. Maybe he'd fenced the horses off his property, planned to claim they weren't his anyway and he didn't have to do anything about them.

That didn't make sense; the Tribe would sell the whole herd to the boneyard, and none of Charley's mustangs would be saved. I couldn't see any horses outside his fences either.

The ground inside them was pretty well torn up, as though a good many head had been through his upper dry-land pasture that week. But where the hell were they?

As I neared the upper fence with its gate leading into Coyote's Ground, I stopped thinking; if I'd thought, I'd have known the answer, and I didn't want to just then. The ground was torn more than down below, and the tracks seemed to lead toward the gate. I didn't even glance in that direction, but instead looked both ways into the trees along the fence, watching for horses. When I reached the top, I turned to gaze back out over the valley. The crowd around Charley's cabin was growing; a slow, steady stream of cars and pickups drove up the dirt road. I couldn't see a horse anywhere.

Finally I turned to the Coyote Gate, concentrating so I wouldn't yet see the ground beyond it, or the chute leading down the mountain. The Gate itself was, if anything, tighter than the last time I'd seen it, but the wire loops holding it closed had been moved out of their grooves and some of the rust on them had flaked off. One loop had been replaced; the wire there was bright and new. When I finally allowed myself to look beyond the gate, I saw the old loop, broken and rusted through, lying where Charley had tossed it out of the way into the brush. And I saw the torn-up earth leading over into Rivers' horse chute down the mountainside.

Charley'd repaired the chute, too, or at least as much of it as I could see from the gate: fresh branches and brush had been pulled up and tied in place, securing the shallow part of the ravine there on the hilltop. Further down it was deeper. I opened the Coyote Gate and walked through, not bothering to close it behind me, and for perhaps ten minutes I followed the chute down. Charley'd restored all Rivers' old barriers where the ravine edge dipped, and he'd even added a new one where the rim had crumbled since we'd repaired this chute before.

I could have followed it all the way to the bottom — the animals had trampled the brush flat, so it was pretty easy walking — but I didn't need to. Charley'd spent the three weeks I'd been advertising his sale rebuilding the chute, fixing the fences back on the ranch, then driving the horses into Rivers' dry pasture and out the Coyote Gate. He'd probably driven a few at a time, then closed the gate behind them and let them find their own way to the bottom. And I suspected he had rebuilt the old gate at the low end, followed the last batch of horses down, and latched it behind them so they couldn't find their way back up the chute. He'd gotten rid of his horses, all right. Put them right back where he'd gotten them. And because there were now laws protecting wild mustangs on federal land, which includes Coyote's Ground, he might just get away with it. None of those horses had been branded, none broken, and none was apt to let a strange man get too close. For that matter, they *were* mustangs; they'd just been removed for a few years from where they belonged, and now that it was safe, they'd come back. If any part of Charley was old man Coyote, he'd kept faith with the earth for certain this time.

I cussed a little, with pleasure, and even allowed myself to laugh as long as no one was around to see, while I walked back up through the chute, avoiding the droppings that littered the ground. Most were drying now; Charley'd probably finished his work a couple of days before, and then spent his time trucking in the beer.

I closed the Coyote Gate behind me. A pretty good party was going on down at Charley's; he'd clean up on beer if I didn't close him down — might even make enough to pay the fine he'd get for selling beer without an auction. As I walked down the hill, I wasn't sure Fisher and I could handle the crowd if I did try to shut things down — would people listen to a deputy with beer on his breath under the orders of a chief who'd put up posters announcing the thing in the first place? Billy White Bull had been right; I was the government man this time, and I hadn't watched myself closely enough.

People were turning toward me as I approached. Some had been standing around for better than an hour, and they were ready for some excitement. One wise-ass called out, "You been checking how many head Charley's got to sell, Snook? Kind of tough to count, ain't they?" Everyone laughed, but not as loud as they might have, and I felt the crowd could turn mean pretty quick, if they decided they didn't like Charley getting away with this while their horses went to the dogmeat man.

Charley'd been sitting on the steps, watching me work my way downhill. Now he stood, walked over to the corral, clambered up, and stood on the next rail down from the top, balancing and waving his arms, calling for quiet. The crowd turned to watch, and I came over to lean against the corral about ten feet away.

"All *right* now," Charley was bellowing. "We got the chief back to witness, and we can get this sale going and over with so we can drink some beer." Somebody toward the crowd's rear — that's where you usually find the yahoos anyway — yelled out, "What the hell's for sale? Postcards?"

Charley held up a hand. "Now, boys, you wouldn't want the officers here to get in trouble for drinking beer when there wasn't a sale, would you?" He gestured over toward the cabin, and all of us followed his pointing arm, saw Skunk Bear and Fisher standing where they could keep an eye on the crowd, but each with an open beer in his hand. They looked a little worried, and neither would meet my eyes. The crowd laughed, not loudly.

I wanted attention away from my officers, so I yelled for everyone to hear, "You're a little short-handed, Charley; want me to lead the first horse into the ring for you?" The crowd turned back to Charley, grinning.

Charley and I were grinning, too, but his was happier than mine. "No, Snook, I'm an honest horse-trader, and I'm gonna go on my reputation and sell these horses sight unseen." He paused for all the horse-traders in the audience to stop laughing at the idea of honest horse-trading. "All right now! So's I can offer you all a better deal, I'm gonna do the auctioneering myself. I'm offering stallions, assorted colors — some assorted right on the horse itself — all pure-blood, special-bred mustangs raised right here on the ranch! All you got to do is go down into the Breaks and catch them! I figure Slippery Ann Creek'd be a good place to look about now!" Slippery Ann is right in the middle of the worst part of Coyote's Ground; it's the only part that's low enough to be swampy. "Bills of sale and everything — an actual legal sale! Be a new experience for some of you boys! Discounts on everything! Any offers? . . . pretty tight crowd here, Snook.

"Mares, then! All colors! Proven breeders, every one! Some with colts, some carrying colts! That's two for the price of one, and the discount on top! Upgrade your stock! You, Pete!" — here he singled out a man who raises real blooded animals, registered quarterhorses — "Pete! One of these mares be just what you need to perk up your bloodline — you'll be the only breeder around offering genuine registered quarterhorse mustangs! Probably corner the market! What do you bid? Call it out now — I know you like to pay top dollar for everythin', but don't be bashful at namin' a low price, this is bargain day! I saw that pickup you're drivin' with the over-sized jockey-box for carryin' cash, so make me an offer! I'm easy today, Pete! What do you say? We're waitin' on you!" He stopped, and everyone waited for poor Pete to speak up.

Now Pete's so damned tight he squeaks, and he's too proud of those quarterhorses to be able to laugh about them. He didn't know what to say, but just stood there, shaking his head, and looking at the ground. Charley tried his best to look disappointed. "You're probably right, Pete — the Feds get you for unfair competition if you cornered the market in pure-blood quarterhorse mustangs. But these folks are sure disappointed — they'd been looking for some real spirited, cut-throat bidding out of you. You can't let them go home with long faces now — maybe you could buy them a beer instead. What do you say, boys? Soon's we're through with this high-spirited bidding war here, old Pete ought to buy a round! Give him a hand and let him know you appreciate it! Anybody opposed? No, Pete, your vote don't count — you're just bein' modest, but we all know you got money, so you might as well spread it around a little! You boys negotiate with Pete after.

"All right! Young stuff — colts that ain't been weaned, all the way up to two-year-olds! Probably win the Kentucky Derby with some of these, and think of the odds you'd get! No takers? What am I bid for any horse, any color, any gender — except geldings! Not a gelding on the place. Well, not a a horse, anyway — can't speak for some of you fellas. Any bids? Last chance coming up — any bid on any animal will be entertained! And then Pete will entertain us all with a round! Going once! Going twice! Going three times! And you've missed the chance of a lifetime! Sale's over! Anybody wants to make a private offer later is out of luck. And now that them deputies of Snook's can drink legal 'cause we've had us a sale, it's time to talk to Pete about that drink — where'd he go anyway? Whose pickup's that goin' down the road? Snook, shouldn't you arrest that man for speeding? Barman, one beer for everybody, in Pete's memory! We'll bill him later. Go get it, boys!"

The crowd rushed for the beer window; no one stuck around to watch Charley jump down from the fence and walk over to me. "That good enough to be legal, Snook?"

I wasn't sure whether I wanted to go along with him or not. "Didn't sell a lot of horses, Charley."

He reached out and grabbed my shoulder. "Hell, we'd just have taken up the whole day leading animals in and out of the ring, while everybody felt worse and worse and loused up the beer sales. This bunch is as happy as if they'd thought of it themselves."

I had to admit it was a happy crowd. And Charley had gotten me off the hook about the beer. What the hell. I turned away, started toward the cabin.

"You better buy me a couple for putting up all those damn posters," I growled over my shoulder.

Charley came shouting, "Hey, bartend! A beer for this man! He worked up a thirst puttin' up posters!" Then, leaning in close so no one could overhear, "But you were wrong, Snook. I did have to repair that damned chute." He pushed his way into the crowd before I could answer, calling back, "This one's on me — he gets one from old Pete, too!"

The crowd closed in around each of us then, slapping Charley on the back, kidding me about the posters. Charley was right; he'd worked the crowd until there were no hard feelings — except maybe Pete's, and he wasn't there to show them.

And it kept on that way; everyone around the Reservation seemed to feel Charley'd done just what they'd have expected from Bill Rivers' grandson, and that of course Charley Many Rivers, or old Bill Rivers, or old man Coyote, or whoever he was, would get away with it. The old people seemed to think the whole thing just proved that the world was, indeed, as they'd always thought it was.

Billy White Bull even told me a Coyote story he said should have warned me what to expect. Once, he said, there was a family which trapped all the buffalo and hid them in a hole in the ground. Then they set up their tipi over the mouth of the hole, so they could watch over it, and they made the people buy buffalo. They could do this thing because their men were strong, fierce warriors, and no one could stand against them. Soon they had almost all the goods in the village, and the people were starving and weeping. Coyote came walking that way, hungry and looking for a hand-out, but the people only wept louder when he begged for food. At first, Coyote thought his hard-luck story had been so good it was causing their sorrow, and he smiled all over inside at the thought of the meal they'd give him when they were able to control themselves again.

But when two days passed and no food appeared, Coyote was hungrier even than he'd been when he arrived, and he finally asked someone what was the matter. It was an old woman he asked, one who was too starved and hungry even to weep any longer, and she told him about the family who had taken the buffalo.

Coyote grew angry then, and he stomped all over the village, talking about what he would do, until he passed by the tipi where the buffalo were hidden and saw how big were the warriors who lived there. Then he became quieter, and finally he approached the old woman again. "Grandmother," he said to her, "I will help you, and maybe I will help everyone. I will be a dish, a lovely dish, and you take me to those people and trade me for meat. Then when they take me inside their tipi, I will do something."

The old woman who was too weak to cry stirred herself then, and took the dish — which didn't surprise her, because this was Coyote and she supposed he could do this sort of thing, even if no tales before then said he could; probably he'd just thought of it for the first time — and she took the dish to those people, and offered it to them for some meat. She drove a hard bargain, and got a hind quarter for it, enough to make soup for the whole village, because she was a good old woman and she knew that others were as hungry as she was, even if she'd gotten weaker from hunger than they had.

This family of buffalo-ranchers took the dish into the tipi, and used it to hold the roast meat for their meal that night. Somehow, the meat was eaten more rapidly this evening than usual, even though everyone claimed not to have had a second helping. The women scolded at that, and said there was no reason to lie about how much they'd eaten, since they had all the buffalo in the world down in the hole behind the fire, but no one would admit to eating more than his share. They became angry, and quarrelled, and went to bed unhappy with one another. Someone noticed the platter quivering once, but thought it was because of the way they were shouting and stomping the ground as they argued.

It was, of course, Coyote laughing at his joke. He was so pleased, in fact, that he almost turned back into himself so he could leap up and shout, "Hoh! I fooled you! Your dish is Coyote!" and run away into the night; the woman had mentioned the hole with the buffalo in it just in time to remind him why he was really there.

After the people were asleep, Coyote the dish managed to slide over to where they'd set a rock over the hole. Then he changed himself into an ant, and crept past the rock into the hole, and there, indeed, were all the buffalo in the world, standing as far as the eye could see, and they weren't happy, either, about living in a hole instead of free on the prairies. Coyote told them to get ready, and when he lifted the rock off to run out as fast as they could, and get out of the tipi and away and never let themselves be captured like that again. Then he crept back out, turned himself into Coyote, and picked up the rock and threw it out through the tipi entrance, tearing the entrance larger. The buffalo came boiling up out of the ground, one after the other after the other, and out through the entrance, past the other tipis, and into the night. The people living in those other tipis had all stayed inside, because with Coyote around you didn't know what might happen, and it was a good thing, because buffalo came out all night long, and someone would probably have been trampled. A few brave men and old grandmothers looked out, and they said it was a thing to see when the tipi started erupting buffalo.

Of course when the buffalo starting running through their home, the buffalo ranchers woke up, and all their warriors reached for weapons and said hard things to Coyote, who was still standing by the hole, enjoying himself. When he saw the weapons, he got scared, and before he thought about it, he said, "I wish you were crows! Crows! And stuck in the smokehole!" And suddenly all the people in the tent drifted upwards to the smokehole, and became very small, with beaks and wings and claws, and white — because crows were white then. Coyote looked up at them, not understanding what he'd done for a moment, and then as pleased as though he'd meant to do it. "Yes," he said to himself, because the buffalo weren't listening; they were just running. "That is a good thing. And there is something else I can do to you, too."

When the buffalo had all run out of the hole, Coyote went to the entrance and called out to the people to bring him wood, and he built a fire, using the greenest pieces, and he smoked the buffalo rancher crows for four days, until they were as black as they could be, and then he let them go, telling them to remember their lesson. He said from now on they should hunt when they were hungry, just like everyone else. Then he told the people in the village to come and take back their things, and to fix him some buffalo meat. Some of the buffalo had hurt themselves running out of the hole, and the people had been able to kill them the next morning right there in the camp.

But the crow buffalo ranchers ever since have hung around where people live, trying to steal food from them, whether from their gardens and fields, or from their drying-racks, so we always have to watch for crows. And no one ever again tried to ranch with buffalo. In fact, when we first saw cattle, we weren't certain it didn't apply to them, too.

So it should have been no surprise to anybody that Charley had turned those horses loose, Billy said. The surprise was that it had taken him so long — or taken his Coyote part so long — to remember that that's what he should do. And if I'd just thought about the old stories the way I should have, I'd have known it, too. But it was maybe a good thing that I hadn't, because then I'd have had to stop him, and that wouldn't have been good. This way, everyone was happy.

Except, I thought now, pulling my horse up and trying

to look around me — realizing that I'd lost my sight almost completely and had better get into the shade — the ranchers who'd been running cattle down in the Breaks. Their cowhands began reporting that the graze was going off too fast; they said a lot of mustangs were down there all of a sudden, eating the fodder they'd leased for their cattle. When we heard about it on the reservation, we just kept quiet; and when the ranchers complained to BLM, the Feds took a look and decided those mustangs must have been hiding in the rougher sections, and the cowboys hadn't noticed them before — which was pretty stupid, but about what a Federal man would think. You can't argue with a government man; he doesn't get enough ideas to be willing to let go of one he does corral.

So BLM told the ranchers they'd have to run fewer cows, since the mustangs were protected by law now and had priority on that land, and they enforced it. Things in Coyote's Ground became about as they'd been before MacDonald had moved cattle in there in the first place, only this time they were likely to stay that way, at least for a while — as long as anything in Coyote's Ground could remain stable. We sure weren't about to tell anyone where those horses had come from. A lot of people think that land should still be ours anyway.

I'd been riding along for some time without paying attention to the trail, thinking instead about Charley's horse auction and Billy White Bull's tales. I was probably still on the right path, assuming that Charley hadn't turned off somewhere, but I couldn't see well enough to look for tracks. The sun was almost directly overhead, and everything reflected it right into my eyes; each flash would stay with me for some minutes, and then the next flash would strike, and even between flashes the world was breaking up into angles. Those angles follow the first dim vision, and after them comes blackness, but for a while yet I'd still be able to see out of my left eye. Once, I remember — I always remember this — I looked in a mirror just before the blackness closed in. Where my face should have been was a collection of angles, broken up to resemble nothing human, with a flowing everywhere — probably, a doctor said when I told him about it, the blood in my own eyes. I had wanted to look in the mirror longer, but couldn't.

I can't call what my mind does after the angles come thinking, because one of the things I lose then is language; I know, somewhere inside my head, what it is I would put into words, but I have no words left, and the images in my mind are like those my eyes bring me from outside. But a sort of sensing continues, without the words and images which otherwise would make me human. And I sensed, then, that Charley's buffalo hunt might not be a hunt at all, but more nearly a herding — or perhaps both at once: a hunt by the part of Charley that was still Charley Many Rivers, and that wanted to kill the buffalo in the old Indian way, and a herding by something unknown to the Charley part, the Coyote part, taking the buffalo away from Sven's buffalo ranch down to Coyote's Ground to turn it loose, like the horses.

Billy White Bull's notion that Charley was Coyote, or at least that a part of him was, seemed right to me then. For years, I'd walked suspiciously around the idea, sniffing at it, kicking my leg up occasionally and pissing on it so I'd be able to find it again, then wandering away for awhile knowing that the piss smell would help me identify it when I came back. Now I was ready to accept the idea, to piss on it not just so I could find it again, but to mark it as mine, within my boundaries.

I needed shade, and I needed it badly. I could hardly stand to look around through the stabbing light. Where I was seemed to be, through the angles, a large piece of open ground, with brush too short to offer much shade. I must have been about half-way between the hills and the river, in one of the large open areas where the ground is less broken. I turned the horse half around, back toward the mountains where there would be trees large enough to shade me. If I gave the animal

98

his head, he'd take me to shade, probably to water as well, one of the streams which run out of the hills through Coyote's Ground. If Coyote had been there, I could have asked him for water, though that was dangerous; once, thirsty, he'd made it rain, forgotten how to make it stop, and nearly drowned before the clouds poured themselves empty. Days and days they'd rained, until all ground was covered, all but the highest hilltops. But there was no rain where I rode, no clouds, only the sun. I closed my eyes, hunched over the saddle horn, hung on and waited.

IV

Coyote's Cave

I KEPT THE HORSE moving, the reins knotted around the saddle horn. Motion, at least, I could still be aware of, though barely, as I receded down within myself, before thought, before sense, before even body to some core that still knew itself as core, as self, without language or understanding. I returned, I think now, to beginnings, and found even there some further depth.

Eventually — or so I think; I had no way of measuring, of saying eventually, or feeling a need to say it; I say it now — eventually I felt shade. The horse kept going, and I hoped it would move toward water.

When finally the animal halted, I could sense its head dropping, the slobbering as it mouthed in water, a coolness in the air that could come only from a stream flowing over rocks. I dismounted, felt my way — not as one normally would feel, but by reaching out with hand or foot until I could reach no further and so knew something was holding me back, whether earth, or rock, or brush, or tree I had no way of telling — felt my way to water, drank, thrust my head under the surface, feeling slight resistance as the water allowed

100

me in, sensing slight pressure in nose, ears, mouth; even my tongue and gums were numb, what other times I would have called "asleep." No sensation but a kind of prickling and absence came through.

I made my way toward more coolness upstream. Once I slipped, found myself lying in the water, and that brought back a tiny sliver of vision, just for a moment. I looked ahead, saw a maze of angles made liquid by the translucent blood flowing through my own eyes, and also saw shifting through the angles an opening out of which the water flowed, a cave that seemed — only seemed, nothing was — large enough for a man, stooping, to enter if he walked in the water. I crawled up the stream, crawled into the cave as my eyes quit on me for good. I couldn't tell if the cave was black or only grey within, but there was a ledge where I could lie just out of the water. I crawled onto it, lay on my back in the cool air, gave myself up completely. As yet I felt no pain, and whatever was still conscious inside me gave over then, slipped away.

There's a story about Coyote and a cave, or at least one version of it is about Coyote. Coyote and Wolf, at the very beginnings, have floated on a raft for days and days without seeing land. Finally they get tired of floating, and start wondering if maybe there isn't some land beneath all that water. Neither can swim, so they persuade Loon, who's been floating alongside, to dive, find mud. Loon tries, almost drowns, but finds nothing. Then the other divers try, but with no more success. Finally Big Turtle tries, and comes back up unconscious, a bit of mud clutched in his claws. Wolf takes it, rolls it into a ball, and it starts growing; soon it pushes them all off the raft and into the water, where Wolf and Coyote discover they can swim a little bit after all. They paddle around, trying to climb onto the ball, and eventually they do. At first, everything is wet and muddy and uncomfortable, and Coyote sits complaining that they were better off on the raft, but Wolf tells him to shut up, soon things will dry out.

And soon things are dry, but Coyote starts complaining that he's hungry. No one listens, because that's what Coyote always does. Coyote complains louder, and soon he's dancing up and down, crying at the top of his voice for food, over and over: "There should be something to eat! There should be food! What kind of a world is this? There ought to be food!"

Just then, with a little crack! a cave opens in the rocks — some of the mud has dried so hard it's become rock — and ants start coming out. Coyote looks at them and says, "Maybe this is food?" He starts licking them up, only some escape him, so there can be ants in the world. Coyote thinks this is a nice, crunchy sort of food, only his tongue gets tired, and he doesn't think he can ever eat enough. Soon he starts complaining again, because other insects are coming out of the cave along with the ants, and some of them aren't very good to eat — the stinkbugs he doesn't like at all, and the bees sting his tongue when he tries a mouthful. So Coyote says, "These things should be larger! They should be larger!" Then shrews, mice, rabbits and other small animals start coming.

Coyote's started to figure things out, and so he lets the small animals pass by. Wolf tells him to try a rabbit, but Coyote says, "No, rabbits look stringy," and ever since, they have been. Coyote gets an idea, and he says, "They should keep getting larger! They should keep getting larger!" Then the animals grow all the way up to antelope, deer, elk, and moose, and Wolf is saying, "Come on now, let's take one of these," and Coyote is saying, "No, let's wait for something really big — I think I can hear it now, so get ready," and they set themselves to jump on the next animal that appears.

They can hear it rumbling up from underground long before it gets there. Coyote decides that he's going to jump the minute its nose sticks out, and he does. Only this time it's Grizzly Bear, who roars when he sees Coyote coming at him, and Coyote almost dies of fright when he sees Bear's teeth and hot red gullet; Coyote thinks he's going to be Bear's dinner, but fortunately he doesn't say it. Instead he cries out, through his fright, "You don't eat Coyotes! You don't eat Coyotes!" Grizzly swats him away and runs off into the trees where no one with any sense will bother him.

Coyote rolls end over end for a while, his nose tucked into his tail so it won't get as badly bruised as the rest of him, and he has a long walk back. When he arrives, Wolf and the others are still rolling around on the ground, laughing at him, howling out, when they can catch their breaths, "You don't eat Coyotes! You don't eat Coyotes!"

Then they hear another rumbling underground. This time even Coyote gets out of the way until he sees what it is. The rumbling comes closer; Coyote sees a great shaggy head with horns approaching the cave mouth; he shrinks back even further, thinking of how good the ants tasted. "Watch out!" he cries, "This one has horns!" and he hides under a rock.

Then the Buffalo runs out of the cave past all those who hide behind the rocks. Wolf starts laughing again, but this time at himself and his friends. Coyote hasn't seen the animal very clearly from under the rock, but he remembers those horns and sees that this one was even larger than the last one. When Wolf says, "That's what I want to hunt," Coyote shakes his head and mutters that the rabbits didn't look so stringy after all, and goes back to eating ants. Only first he stands in front of the cave and shouts, "No more! No more! We're running out of room for the big ones!" Then he listens for a while, doesn't hear anything else coming, and trots off, proud of himself for putting an end to the rush of new animals. There weren't any more to come after the Buffalo anyway — but Coyote never does figure that out.

Years later, Billy White Bull says, Coyote comes back to that same cave, and moves into it, thinking it looks large and comfortable. The cave, Billy says, is the one Coyote lives in down in Coyote's Ground, but I was too far gone to worry about it.

In the next few hours I awoke occasionally, first to blackness, then to angles in a dim world, followed by blank spots where angles had been, and finally to vision — clear, sharp, stronger than any other time — and pain with every heartbeat. The doctors say these attacks are rather simple physically, though they aren't sure what triggers them: in the the early stages, blood vessels into forward parts of my brain close, the flow slows to a trickle, enough to keep things alive, not enough to let them function. Later the process reverses and the vessels open again. Blood flows easily, but since my heart has kept pumping the whole time at its usual rate, there's a backlog of pressure that hasn't had any place to go. My own blood, then, comes flooding through my brain, and the veins expand, pressuring everything. The first pain is always enough to bring me to, briefly, before the blood re-awakens my senses, before I feel the pain as completely as I will later.

The pain builds quickly; pain is always the first sense to recover, and it keeps on for hours, peaking quickly, then slowly leaving me as the crest passes, the flow levels out. During that time, my senses are sharpened, cleared; I per-ceive more fully than at any other.

I always hope the attack might turn into a vision like the old-timers had, but so far none has. I seem to drift away from this world, just as they did, but I don't break through into any other; instead, I hang in limbo, stay there until the blood starts flowing again.

At first, then, I can't bear to move, to look around, to hear anything but the softest of sounds; later, as the pain re-cedes, the pleasure I take in my senses almost compensates. It comes nearer to compensating as the pain leaves, even though the acuteness with which I move through the world also leaves.

So when I first opened my eyes to discover I could see again, I didn't keep them open for long, nor did I try to sit up for a while. It was all I could take to move my eyes and head to see exactly where I was, and even the gurgling of the water as it flowed past my rock, the occasional splash and reflection of the cave's dim light, were almost too much to bear.

I could think clearly, though I still didn't have as many words as I'd have liked; my memory for words is last to recover, and sometimes I find myself lost in the beauty of something I can't yet name. I could think it must still be daylight outside, because of the dim light in the cave, late afternoon or early evening, too late, by the time I could endure the jolt of my own feet striking the ground, to say nothing of the jolt of a horse's walking, to get back on the trail again. I'd be best off to stay where I was, try to eat something after a bit, get an early start in the morning. Surprisingly, the cave's air seemed only slightly moist, just enough to be pleasant, not damp as the stream flowing through it should have meant. I lay for a while, simply enjoying the feel of the air on my face and hands, the taste of it in my nose and mouth, its coolness in my lungs.

My arms and legs tingled as I came back into touch with them. My right arm would have a little numbness for a time, but by morning it would be fine, and even before then I could use it. My right leg would give more trouble — it wouldn't want to support me, and I'd have to stump around carefully.

Coyote had trouble with his arms, at first. He wasn't sure what they were, so he sat down to explore. He held the left one out in front, looked it over carefully, tried moving it; it moved when he told it to, all right. The fingers were especially interesting — he admired the way they tapered, then noticed one of them didn't taper but was blunter, shorter, opposed to the first four, and could touch each of the others. That was interesting, too; without thinking much about it, he brought his right hand over to take hold of that short finger, maybe stretch it a little, push it back where it should be, straight like the others, when — wait a minute!

There was another set of fingers, and another short one! He sat for a while, puzzled, moving the fingers back and forth, wiggling the short one, glancing around occasionally to see if there were any more of these things lurking behind him. He wasn't certain which hand he should use to touch the other with, and finally just rubbed them together. They both seemed to be his, and they followed orders. That was good; he seemed to remember he'd found a newly-dead buffalo nearby, and hadn't been able to tear the tough hide away with his teeth — maybe these hands would help. He took up two sharp rocks, and set out for where the buffalo was.

But Coyote hadn't learned to use his new hands very well, and they kept getting in each other's way. Soon each hand had gathered a little pile of meat, and they were ripping and tearing at the buffalo with the sharp rocks, so that neither could get any more. Then the hands grew angry, and each began to wave its sharp stone at the other. Coyote thought that was great fun; oh, I'll get to see a fight! he thought.

Each hand began to cut and slash at the other, and soon there were gashes up and down both arms, with blood running down and making the sharp rocks slippery and hard to hold. About that time Coyote began to realize that something wasn't right — all that cutting and slashing hurt. Every time one hand cut the other, Coyote could feel it! He looked hard at the right hand, followed the arm back up to a shoulder located right next to his own head; when he bent his head that way, it felt like he was connected to the shoulder. And when he followed the other arm up, he found a shoulder on that side, too, and when he bent his head, that shoulder also felt connected — and then he felt all the cuts and bruises the two hands had caused, and with a great howl, he threw down the sharp stones and ran away from there, crying and pitying himself, hungry as always.

I was getting a bit hungry myself; I'd slept the day through, hadn't eaten since breakfast back at Charley's cabin. I stood on the ledge, bending to keep my head from bumping on the rock above, and tested my leg. The limp wouldn't be too bad, and I could use both hands, though the right one was a little uncertain yet. When you go without feeling in an arm for a while, you lose track of just where it is, or whether it's doing what you want it to do, unless you watch it the whole time, and you keep forgetting to watch it. I backed out of the cave, using my good left leg as a sort of brace, getting my feet wet again, but not having any real trouble. The stream wasn't swift, only a couple of feet wide, maybe eight inches deep.

It looked to be early evening. The trees to my west — the cave opened to the south — blocked my view of the horizon, but the colors on the few high-riding clouds said the sun was setting. The horse had stayed close to the cave, where there was grass and shade and the water was coldest. He came up to me now, a bit hesitant, and I unsaddled, hobbled him, and removed the bridle for the night. Bridle and saddle I hung on a branch where nothing could get at them, and the saddle bags and bedroll I took back inside the cave, slipping and sliding on the bad leg, carefully bracing with my right arm while the left held the bags and bedroll.

I dumped my gear on the rock where I'd slept, clambered up and sat to catch my breath. Light in the cave was dim at best, and with the sun going down it was fading fast. I took a flashlight from one of the bags and directed it around the cave. It wasn't large — twenty, maybe thirty feet deep, sloping upwards into the mountain and getting higher as it went. Up above seemed to be a crack that let in some light, though not directly — that is, the crack didn't seem to go right straight up, or at least I couldn't find an angle that would let me see the sky through it. I could feel a slight draft coming past me from the cave's mouth; probably the crack drew air up and out, which would explain why the cave was cool and moist, but not damp. About ten feet in, the cave widened enough to make a nice spot for a campfire and bedroll; the stream seemed to come from under the wall opposite the rock on which I sat, and it ran along that wall to the cave's mouth, leaving the center dry.

I hauled my saddlebags and bedroll to the wide spot, then crawled back outside to gather enough wood for a small fire. There was plenty of down timber, old stuff and dry, so I went back a second time to haul in some small logs; if the cookfire didn't smoke up the cave too much, I'd keep warm that night.

I found a small depression in the rock, moved some loose stones to make a ring, and got my fire going. Then I took the coffee pot out and filled it, sliced some bacon into a pan, let it sizzle for a couple of minutes, dumped a can of beans in and sat back while supper cooked. Staring into a fire always leaves me a little night-blind when I look away, and besides the flames were too bright just then, so I looked around me instead. That fire lit the cave more than I'd have expected; there may have been something in the rock to reflect a little light, or it may have been the sharpness my eyes always have after an attack.

Off to my left I saw something wedged in between two rocks, with a slight overhang above. It was probably the nest of some small animal or other, but so far I hadn't noticed any tracks or droppings, certainly no old bones or hair as there would have been if anything lived and ate here. The nest was likely an old one, but for lack of anything else to do while the coffee boiled, I got up and limped over to take a look.

The rocks with their overhang sat toward the back of the cave, on the wall opposite the stream. When I turned my flashlight beam on what I thought was the nest, I found instead the skin of some long-dead animal, dusty and even a little moth-eaten. For a moment I thought something had crawled in there to die, and I reached out, intending to toss the thing out the cave mouth. There was room to stoop under the overhang, even for someone of my height.

Whatever it was had been dead long enough to have dried out; there was no odor, even when I leaned over it. I took hold with my right hand, keeping the flashlight in my left, but realized, even without any sense of touch in the hand lifting the skin, that I didn't have hold of the mummified remains of some dead thing, but instead gripped a hide with something wrapped inside. I eased it back down, used my right hand to place the flashlight between my left arm and body so it would still give me some light, and eased both arms under the wrapping, the way I would a baby — carefully, convinced dropping it would be a disaster. The thing was light, but not so light as to be empty skin; definitely something was wrapped inside. I thought it might have been left here by some old-time Indian who hadn't been able to come back for it; perhaps it would be something the Museum could use, and by offering it I could persuade them to drop charges against Charley once I'd caught him. Because that, too, is part of my job as I see it — to keep peace, and when it's broken to restore it, and something approaching harmony with it. If the Museum pieces came back undamaged, and if this hide contained something the Museum would want in addition to what Charley'd taken, then the staff might not feel too badly if we kept Charley here, on probation, instead of sending him off to prison. When we send a man away, it diminishes the Tribe; and finally the Tribe counts beyond everything.

I'm not certain when I began thinking this way; it may have been when Billy White Bull told me the old people thought I'd acted like a Peace Chief, or it may have been later, after I'd become Chief of Tribal Police and started seek-seeking out Billy's advice. Billy's always said Police Chief is a mistake, that the white fella who first wrote that title couldn't bring himself to come any closer to Peace Chief.

I felt a tingle, almost a jolt, in my right arm, as though I'd come into contact with something sufficient to drive through my dormant nerves; and as I lifted the bundle, I felt uneasy, unsure, as though somehow I should leave it alone. Fleas, I thought, maybe even ticks; probably the thing was infested with bugs — but those I could brush off. My uneasiness grew, and I was glad to lay the thing beside the fire where I could get a good look at it.

It was certainly a man-made bundle — an old animal hide, wrapped around something. Looking closely, I couldn't see any bugs. I began to open it, slowly and carefully, not to harm anything inside. Still, opening it felt wrong — as though whoever it had belonged to would still, years after he must have died, be furious I'd dared meddle. The hide was wrapped several times; I'd unrolled two layers when I stopped.

The coffee was boiling; I poured myself a cup and moved the pot away from the fire, where it would keep hot but not boil. Then I sat back, a ways from the bundle, sipping my coffee, thinking about what I'd found.

It could be some old-time warrior's personal Medicine Bundle — a sort of individual version of the Holy Bundle that hung in the tribal museum. Inside I would find the things his vision had shown him — the skin, or part of the skin, of some animal or bird which had spoken to him, perhaps his personal sacred pipe and paints, whatever else he'd seen. In the old days, everyone owned such a bundle; usually it was hung in the tipi, or tied to your saddle if you were traveling far — on a war party or long buffalo hunt, let's say. No one carries such bundles now; no one has visions.

I shouldn't say no one. Some of the old people have bundles from visions which came when they were young, and maybe some of them do still have visions — you hear rumors, but of course they can't talk about it. And you hear that some of the southwest tribes hold the old ways, but I don't know if they ever carried medicine bundles or not. For us, the bundle was, in a way, almost a personal altar — but only in a way. When you needed to pray, you'd open the bundle, singing a song you'd been taught in your vision, and dress yourself in what you found within, the way the vision had shown you; you'd wear part of the hide of whatever bird or animal had appeared to you, perhaps carry on a thong around your neck a stone like one you'd seen in the vision; you'd paint yourself as the vision had instructed, and you'd go out alone to pray, still singing your sacred song. That way, by partly recreating the vision, you'd help it happen again. If anyone else opened your bundle, the power would leave it; but this bundle's owner must have died long before, so I couldn't harm his power now. Besides, the bundle before me seemed pretty large to be someone's private medicine bundle.

I set the cup down and returned to the bundle. Carefully, slowly, uncertainly, I unrolled it once more; I could tell that after the hide had been wrapped around whatever was inside, it had been wrapped once separately around something else, and then wrapped three times around the whole again. In the fourth wrapping from the outside, I uncovered a pipe.

I knew I wasn't going to look further. I recognized that pipe — not from seeing it before, because I hadn't, and I doubted any but the oldest had, but from hearing about it ever since I could remember. What I'd heard I won't repeat; it's not for a man without a vision to describe that pipe. But I'd heard enough to know that it was old, old beyond memory of any time when it hadn't existed, part of the Tribe's lost Medicine Bundle, the Bundle that, when returned to us, would make us whole again, the mate to the Holy Bundle hanging in the Museum.

For a time I didn't move, but just knelt there in the cave, staring at the pipe. I was thankful I hadn't touched it directly, had handled it only through the skin which protected it from hands such as mine. To see it might be allowed; in the old days, it had been brought out occasionally during Tribal ceremonies, or at times of great uncertainty when the old men would smoke and pray and talk. But even that must be done with the proper ceremony, with prayer and fasting and songs, and only by the Keeper of the Holy Bundle. The pipe was a beautiful thing, carved in ways no one can carve now, untouched by time except that its color had deepened and mellowed through the years. After a while — if time existed in that presence — I carefully rewrapped the pipe into the Bundle, lifted it even more carefully than I had before, and carried it back to its resting-place under the ledge. I placed it firmly among the stones where it had been, and backed away.

I nearly backed into my campfire. The beans and bacon were starting to burn, so I took them from the fire, found a fork, and began to eat, directly from the pan. My eyes were returning more nearly to normal now, and I could see the Bundle only as a dim shape in the cave's dim light.

So the old Keeper hadn't given his Bundle to an anthropologist after all; the other version of that story was the true one, that he'd taken it down to the wild lands along the river and hidden it in a cave, to be found again when the Tribe was ready to care for it. The anthropologist story had kept fools and collectors from searching the Breaks to find this cave where the stream kept the air moist, just as in the Museum, so the Bundle wouldn't become dry and brittle, while the crack above kept the air from being too moist, so the Bundle wouldn't rot. I knew I wasn't the man to find it, or to care for it; the man for that would be led here by a vision, not by the nerve-storms I'd always hoped might someday be prelude. But I could do one thing: I could go to Billy White Bull and tell him what I'd seen, so he and the old people could know that the Bundle had not passed beyond us, that someday the right man could come here and reclaim it for the Tribe. This night I would sleep near the Holy Bundle, and perhaps I would, after all, be allowed a vision of my own.

I cleaned up my cooking gear, lay three logs with their ends in the fire, rolled out my sleeping bag, then crawled out of the cave for a last look around before I stretched out. My horse was grazing quietly near the stream, as I'd expected — he wouldn't go far with hobbles on. It was a quiet night, clear, the stars bright and sharp overhead, the moon not yet up. Even in the starlight I could see well, better than in the cave because the outside light was uniform, not the bright and shadow light of the campfire. My right arm had only a little numbness, as though I'd lifted with it all day and now it was too tired to do more; my leg was coming back nicely. By morning I'd be in good shape, this sense-sharpness still mine for a day or two, long enough to catch up with Charley and that buffalo. I sat on a rock, looking out at the world for a while, feeling incomplete and earthly, wanting to be where the Bundle was, and yet half afraid. Perhaps, I thought, I should sleep outside.

I would want to ride for Billy White Bull first thing in the morning, but I knew better. Fisher and Sam would be wondering what had happened to me, and if they'd caught up with Charley during the day I'd spent in the cave, by now they'd be organizing a search for a lost police chief. Billy would have to wait until I'd finished with Charley, one way or another. That Bundle had been hidden safely for better than forty years; it could stay where it was another day or two, and then the old people could decide what to do about it.

I almost expected to find Charley hanging around the cave — certainly the man Thunder Boy described could have been seeking a vision, or acting on one he'd already had. Yet Charley shouldn't have recognized a vision if he'd had one; Bill Rivers had raised him in the newer Metis way — farms left each summer for the buffalo hunt, dances led by Catholic priests, changing from the French and Indian pasts into some third thing neither would have recognized. Sometimes you hear that one day we'll all be Metis, one grey, homogenized race that has lost all its pasts by trying to save only the little which can live with machines.

But there are things in Charley all his own, too, not part of any past Bill Rivers would have taught him — his carving most of all. When I'd watched him whittle a stick into kindling, before he'd driven his mustangs into Coyote's Ground, his knife-work hadn't gone beyond what was useful for building fires. Sometime after he lost the horses he took to carving most of each day.

At first, I think, he spent his days looking out over the empty valley, imagining the horses which no longer ran there, until the memory came to seem distant, something he'd dreamed. Next he must have tried his hand at drawing those horses before he lost them entirely, and found he was a fair hand at pictures. Even pictures wouldn't have satisfied him; a finished drawing would lie there, fooling him into thinking it had depth, weight, substance, until he touched it and discovered nothing but paper, flat on the table. And then, I think, he began to carve.

His first carvings couldn't have looked like much: blunt, blocky figures wooden as the down timber he'd failed to transform. For tools he'd have only jack-knife, for material whatever wood he picked up among the trees: pine from the hills around his valley, cottonwood along the river. He began to hang around the bars, listening to known carvers, hoping they'd talk about their tools, the woods they liked. Being Charley, he didn't ask questions or join their conversations; instead he sat nearby, pretending disinterest as he drank along and quietly, his ears cocked for anything they might reveal. He was buying tools, then — not here in town, where we might have heard what he was up to, but up the road a ways, at a hobby shop. Sometimes he'd follow a carver into a hardware store, buy one of whatever he'd seen the carver take, or even pick up and handle. He made some mistakes: a steak knife whose blade he'd seen a carver test before making the purchase, Charley not knowing the knife had been on a list the man's wife had written.

We didn't know Charley had started carving, even when he he took a sweeping job at the local bronze foundry. That foundry's a tribal project, started with some Bureau money but now able to support itself, a half-dozen foundrymen, and the best of our local carvers. There workmen cast a mold around an original of wood or clay, and use the mold in turn to cast a wax model. The artist works on the model to sharpen any detail that hasn't come clear, then he and the workmen cast a second mold of some stronger material around the wax. When they heat the second mold, the wax melts out, and they can refill the mold with bronze. Later, when the bronze has cooled, workmen reuse the mold — these molds are in two parts, unlike the first mold, which breaks away from the wax model — to make as many as twenty copies, then break the mold so no more copies can be made, and return the original to the artist.

Their equipment doesn't look like much — most of their furnaces were made out of fifty-gallon oil drums — but the statues go to dealers all around the west, sell for three hundred and more each. Cowboy art they call this back east, Charley Russell and Frederick Remington imitations. But even after the dealer and the foundry take their shares, a single original can net an artist as much as six thousand, though two is more likely for beginners, and may take two years to come in. A couple of our local artists have reputations now that sell out an edition in six months, at top prices.

Charley went to work at the foundry in the middle of the worst winter we'd had in some time. The snow kept coming, piling up so cattle bogged down and starved to death, snowplows couldn't clear the back roads before the next storm came in, the February thaw didn't come. Spring was late by three weeks or more, and when it finally arrived, the country was dotted with dead cattle and horses. Fence-lines, where drifts had been deepest, were marked by the bodies of grouse and pheasant which had burrowed into the early, smallest drifts, beaten out hollows with their wings where body heat would keep them alive, then been trapped inside by the next snowfall, buried too deeply to beat their way to fresh air and sunlight. The wild horses in Coyote's Ground thinned out, the oldest, youngest, and weakest dead in the snow. Charley had stopped cutting the hay Bill Rivers left him, allowing it to grow wild and the fences separating it from Coyote's Ground to fall, so mustangs, deer, even rabbits and other small game could get at it. Some of the mustangs came back into his valley, just for the winter, but he couldn't do anything for them, and in mid-winter he drove away from their slow dying. The job at the foundry seemed, to the rest of us, simply a way to get through the winter, and perhaps an excuse as well to keep from going back to the ranch until the dying winter was over. Once he'd left the valley, drifts would keep him from returning until spring.

Charley did his job well enough at the foundry, but mostly he spied on the artists as they worked on wax models or even on originals. That winter he lived in a hotel room over one of the bars, and during those months he didn't carve, didn't buy tools — or if he bought tools, he kept them in the trunk of his car where the hotel janitor wouldn't see them and gossip around town. It's the kind of hotel that doesn't have maid service, just a janitor who sweeps hallways and rooms once a week, while the proprietor's wife changes sheets every now and then. Some say she only moves the sheets from room to room, washes them a couple of times a year if they need it.

When spring came, Charley didn't move back to the ranch until the snow had been out of the hills for over a month and the worst of the death-stench was gone, and even then he stayed in town most week-nights. He'd begun, I'd guess, to borrow tools from the foundry, taking them home Fridays and bringing them back early Mondays before anyone else showed up. Weekends he spent carving in his cabin or out front on the steps. As it turned out, his work was all of horses — the mustangs as he imagined them, not as the stunted, inbred animals they really were even after the winter cleaned out the worst among them. Careful breeding might have produced the horses Charley carved, but actual wild horses never could. Even in the few statues he did of starving, dying animals it was clear that each horse had been strong and healthy before winter took a hand.

We knew nothing of all this until one night he got to

116

drinking in the bar below his hotel room and began talking of how poor even the best artists at the foundry really were, boasting that his work was better, he could make them all look foolish. Word got around, and two days later one of the local artists came storming in where Charley was sweeping and challenged him to prove it, to bring in something for casting and be shamed in front of the whole crew. For a moment the other workers thought there was going to be a fight; they said later Charley crouched for a moment, looked as though he were about to spring out at the other man, and then he straightened, slowly, and simply said all right, he'd bring something in the next morning.

That night he didn't show up at the hotel, or in any of the bars where the janitor was telling people he hadn't shown up. Everyone had a fine time talking and laughing, speculating whether he'd taken off for Canada or Los Angeles, whether he'd ever show his face around the reservation again after making such a boast. Billy White Bull, who would have known all about it somehow — these old people seem to get the news almost before it's happened, as though finally there's only one mind underlying all of us out here, and they alone are fully part of it, the rest of us trying to grow into a fuller hearing — Billy would have said they should have known better, that Coyote always finds some way to make his boasts come true, even if he has to trick someone else into carrying them out by doing the things he can't do, like all the times he tricked Bear into using the magic Coyote was pretending to duplicate to feed Coyote and all his relatives. Billy's worry would have been another one: what the Coyote part of Charley might do, once it started carving things again. That would have scared the hell out of Billy — and it did; he told me of it later — so he'd have spent the night smoking, praying, and watching in the direction of Charley's ranch and Coyote's Ground to see if he could tell what was happening down there.

As it turned out, nothing much went on at Charley's

place, except that he spent the night choosing the best from among his carvings. The next morning the foundry was crowded, and would have been even more crowded if the foreman had let in anyone but the artists who'd heard of Charley's boast and came to see what would happen. Charley had arrived early and gone to sweeping, as though he didn't have a thing on his mind but dust, and he swept until finally the man who'd challenged him came strutting over to laugh. Then he set the broom aside, went to his locker, and came back with a carving of a mustang stallion and a wolf, the stallion rearing over the cowering wolf, anger and triumph in every muscle, the wolf with one paw already smashed, wanting now only to escape, its death large in every line of its shrinking body. The artist who'd issued the challenge stood for a while holding the statue, turning it over and over, searching out every flaw in the piece, while the other artists and the foundry crew gathered to look over his shoulder. Charley took up the broom and went back to his sweeping. Finally the artist handed it to the foreman, not saying anything, cocking his head slightly, raising his eyebrows, nodding.

While the onlookers passed the statue around, the challenger walked over to where Charley swept and pretended not to know anything was happening. There were, the artist said, some parts of the statue that wouldn't show up well in casting; if Charley'd like, he'd show him what they were. Charley still didn't speak, but walked into the crowd, rescued the statue, took it to a workbench and turned to the artist again, waiting. They worked over the statue for a couple of hours, then took it to have the first mold formed around it.

The process from carving to finished statue takes several days, what with heating and cooling in each stage. Charley came in each day to sweep as though nothing had happened, but each evening he went back out to the ranch where no one could talk to him about it. On the last day, he cleaned the foundry so completely that no one dared to set a tool down for fear Charley would seize it, hang it in its proper place on the walls; one man still claims he brushed some wax chips off a bench and Charley caught them before they hit the ground. When the mold came off, no one said anything for a while; then the foreman walked over to Charley and fired him. You're wasting your time with that broom, he said. I want you out making more statues. We'll run twenty of these at three hundred each; you'll get a third, more or less, on each one we sell. And the artist who'd challenged him said he'd buy the first beer.

Charley didn't seem to hear them; he was staring at the statue as though he'd never seen it before, and he kept staring until the foreman put it in his hands, told him to take it home and keep it, since it was his first.

Part of Charley's boast wasn't true: he wasn't the best carver working at the foundry, but he was good enough, and continues good enough, to pull down three- to five-hundred on each statue, even though he doesn't carve anything but mustangs — you can only sell so many mustangs. But he makes a nice living from it, and doesn't do any other kind of work these days. And all that carving continues to worry Billy White Bull something awful.

Billy sees the whole winter as more evidence that part, at least, of Charley Many Rivers was really Coyote. Only Coyote, Billy would say, only Coyote who can live on anything would have turned the death of that winter into new life, into his carvings, into, finally, the way he made a living. Everyone else tends to die in the midst of death; Coyote alone thrives on it, dines as well on carrion as on fresh meat. Coyote alone can turn anything into the materials of his life. But what if he started making those statues come to life? That carving worries Billy.

I was tired, my head ached, my leg wasn't right yet; I needed sleep more than anything else, or so I thought. Maybe that thought was the reason nothing came to me in my sleep, even though I'd crawled into the bag with the Holy

Bundle only a few feet away.

I awoke early the next morning, the cave already dimly lighted. At first I thought I'd only dreamed the Bundle, but it was wedged in the rocks as before. I didn't approach it; that would be for someone else, after I'd told Billy White Bull where it could be found. Instead, I made a quick breakfast, kicked the ashes from my fire into the stream, washed and packed my cooking gear, hauled the sleeping and saddle bags out of the cave, and went to look for my horse.

My senses weren't working as well as the night before, but still everything was sharp and clear enough almost to hurt in the bright sun, and my arm and leg were strong again. I breathed deeply, rolling the pine scent around in my nostrils and mouth, enjoying the textures which made up that scent. I could hear insects moving in the grass, could hear the slight whoosh air made past the wings of a hawk not too far above, and it was a simple matter to locate my horse by the sound of his breathing. He came a bit hesitantly, as though not quite certain of me — or perhaps I simply saw all the parts of his motion, the little stops and starts, the slight variations I'd usually have missed.

My saddle and bridle had gone untouched in the tree. I ran my fingers over the leather texture no more than was necessary to saddle and bridle the horse, to tie my sleeping and saddle bags on, to mount up. I took a last careful look around to be certain I'd recognize the place again, reminded myself to look back every few hundred feet. Landscape changes with your angle, and I didn't want to lose any part of the way back to the cave and the Bundle.

I rode south along the stream, planning to stay down in the brush along the creek bottom until I was back in the area I'd been in yesterday, then let Sam catch sight of me. I would claim to have spent the night there after getting dizzy from the sun and going to sleep in the shade of some brush; that would be why he hadn't been able to see me before. Besides, there was even a slight chance I might come across the buffalo's tracks in the mud along the stream bed; the old bull might have chosen this as the nearest water. He'd sure have been thirsty after the run he'd made.

Somewhere behind me I could hear Sam's airplane approaching from the north, as he returned to start another day's hunt, so I took the radio from my pack, hung it from the saddle horn and turned it on. The static was bad as usual, but that morning I could separate the sounds, understand Sam and Fisher through the static as they tried to talk to one another. I hoped they were still searching for Charley and the buffalo, and weren't down there just to hunt for me.

Sam provided the answer quickly enough. He called back to the base station to report that he was approaching Coyote's Ground and would first locate Fisher, then begin to look for both me and the buffalo. He'd let them know as soon as he'd found Fisher. I stopped under a small cottonwood until he'd flown over, heading south and east. Then I heard Fisher give his radio a try.

"Bird One, this is Mobile Two. I hear you, but haven't seen you yet. Do you read me? Any sign of anything moving? I haven't picked the trail up. No sign of Snook, either. They've all disappeared, as near as I can tell. Do you read me?"

Sam cut in then, reporting back to the base station. "Base, this is Bird One. I see Fisher; he's trying to talk to me, but the noise is too bad. He's signaling now — he's lost the trail still, and he's alone, so I guess he hasn't had any sign of Snook either. If we don't see Snook this morning, I think you'd better get some more men down here; he may be in trouble. We're covering the area between Slippery Ann and Cottonwood creeks now, and we'll keep moving east, since that's the direction they were headed. Snook could be behind us somewhere, so I'll make my loops wide enough to cover the area we went through yesterday and watch for him there, too. Bird One out."

I couldn't hear the reply from the base station; too many hills between us. But I did hear Fisher give it one more try.

"Bird One, this is Mobile Two. Can't hear you for static, but maybe you can read me. I'll keep heading south and east, see if I can't pick up something along the creeks. They had to cross somewhere. And I'll try to stay out of the brush as much as I can, so you don't lose me, too. Out."

So Fisher was south of me, and probably east, judging from where I could hear the airplane's motor noise change as it banked and turned over him, signaling that Sam, too, hadn't seen anything yet. In another hour or so I'd be south enough to ride up where I could let myself be seen, so Sam wouldn't call for more men. I didn't want a whole posse riding around down there, confusing things.

My hour was nearly up, and I was thinking about riding out of the brush and mosquitoes to higher ground above the creek bed when I saw tracks: a single buffalo, crossing the creek, grazing for a while before moving east out of the coulee.

The animal had veered north to the trees, the cool shade and the stream, just as I had. From the looks of his tracks, he'd been walking slowly, grazing as he moved, had either lost Charley or been far enough ahead to think he had. And I was safe, now; Fisher and Sam had lost both the buffalo and Charley, seemed in fact to have gotten ahead of them to the east, and I would claim to have been on the trail all along. That would give me something to kid Fisher about, and I looked forward to it.

I followed the tracks across the stream, up the slope on the far side. The animal had trotted upslope after walking along the stream bed. I expected it to resume walking at the crest, but it hadn't; instead had kept trotting, had even broken occasionally into a run, if I could judge from the tracks, and that morning I could. The running puzzled me, but a quarter mile further on I came across a shod horse, surely Charley's, which had approached from the south. I took time out to backtrack; he'd been following the buffalo, but pretty far back. While the tracks I'd found first were fairly fresh, and all of Charley's were fresh, the buffalo's tracks further downstream had dried completely. It might have grazed most of a day before Charley caught up.

I had no way of knowing whether he'd gotten a look at the bull this time, though I suspected he had because his horse had run along the trail for a while after they joined — not long, however; I'd guessed his horse was pretty well worn down, and the buffalo had rested long enough to be able, once again, to outrun him easily. Finally the shod hooves followed the buffalo at a walk, and I followed at a trot; they were a few hours ahead of me, but my horse had a day's rest, and I might catch up to Charley, at least.

In another quarter-mile I got a surprise: a horse-pulled two-wheeled cart joined the trail and Charley's tracks disappeared. That news stopped me cold for a moment. Who else could be out here? Fisher sure as hell wasn't in a cart, and there hadn't been any third person with Many Rivers and Thunder Boy. Had Charley run into somebody during the time we'd lost his trail? By now, Thunder Boy should be taking it easy in front of the hospital's air-conditioner, if they hadn't thrown him out yet. Would he have come back down here and dug up an old cart somewhere, gotten back in the chase that way because his ankles wouldn't let him ride a horse? I couldn't believe it, not after the last I'd seen of Thunder Boy. But who, then? And where the hell would a two-wheeled half-breed cart have come from down here?

Because that's what it must be: a two-wheeled Red River half-breed cart, down from the old Metis country in Canada. I'd seen carts like that, with their square box and pairs of tall, solid wooden wheels — no niceties like spokes, just a single slab of wood rounded into a wheel, a hole cut through the center for the axle. There were still a few around when I was a kid, left over from when the Metis fled south after the second rebellion. Farmers and ranchers near the reservation preferred buckboards, and so did those of our people with loads to carry, but Metis had always preferred these two-wheeled carts; they used them not on roads, but cross-country, trading with their Indian relatives or going after buffalo, where the two large wheels handled the rough terrain better than anything with four could hope. Down here in Coyote's Ground I wouldn't have believed even a Red River cart could get through, but this one had, judging from the direction its tracks came, and through the roughest part of the country, too. Though the country didn't seem as rough that day as it usually does.

I turned off, followed for a while the cart tracks south from where they had come, but that wasn't telling me much. Charley's horse had seemed tired; I wanted to gain time on him while I could. When I turned back toward the main trail, I held a fast pace, as fast as I thought my horse could keep up; I was worried now. That cart looked like Charley planned to kill and butcher the old bull, use the cart to haul the meat just as Bill Rivers would have done up in Canada. Billy White Bull would have insisted that Bill Rivers would be the driver, but I didn't want to go that far until I'd seen him.

Where the trails joined I paused again, long enough to listen hard to the land ahead. Those old Red River carts made a terrible amount of noise; the Metis didn't make anything fancy, like bearings, and so the wheels were driven onto the axle, and the axle turned in its mountings with nothing but a little grease to ease the friction. I remember that just one cart made a racket that hurt to listen to, the wood screaming its way along; fifty or so of them would have been unbearable. It was that screaming I paused to listen for before I started on the trail again, but I heard nothing I shouldn't have heard, even as keen as my ears were that morning. Perhaps this cart wasn't as noisy as most because its axle had been freshly greased; along the wheel tracks I could see drops melting in the sun.

Those Red River carts were buffalo-hunting carts, all right; the women drove them across the prairie to follow the men on their buffalo-runners after the herd, arriving while the first bodies were still hot from the chase. The men marked each animal they killed, and their families would come racketing up, women, girls, boys too young to hunt would jump down and go to skinning and butchering. Each family drove several carts, some for meat and some for hides, or at least those hides which weren't used to wrap meat from the sun. The hunt continued until all the carts were full, and then the whole town — except the very old and young, who stayed in Red River to water the gardens and feed the chickens — would camp for a few days while the women dressed the meat out properly, worked the hides so they'd keep for tanning back in Red River.

That big fall buffalo hunt was one reason they didn't need much pasture land on their farms — just enough to keep their cart-horses and buffalo-runners, with maybe a couple of milk cows and a steer or two or a couple of hogs for variety. They were still a buffalo people, those old Metis, though they'd settled into square cabins on rectangular ranches in little towns sprawling along the rivers. If there was a Red River cart following Charley through Coyote's Ground, maybe he'd not gone all the way back to Indian in this buffalo hunt, but only to Metis; and in that case, who could tell what it might all mean?

In any case, and whatever it might mean, I had to catch Charley. I followed the trail at a fast trot; with buffalo tracks, shod hooves, and a cart all rolling along before me it was easy enough. I could hear Sam and Fisher try to talk to each other, though not often; they knew they wouldn't hear through the static. Before long I expected Sam to fly back over my way, and now that I was out in the open he'd see me immediately. Once I'd signaled that I was on Charley's trail, Sam would signal Fisher to move north to cut Charley off, and he might even be able to spot the buffalo from the air. It didn't look to me as though things would take long now.

But it didn't work out that way. Sam flew over twice in the next couple of hours, both times to the south but near enough to have spotted me if he'd looked my way, without giving any sign. Well, that was all right, too; the farther along the trail I could travel, the better my story would sound later. And I was moving right along; this was no slow trail to pick out.

I'd been moving rapidly, not paying terribly close attention to the ground in front of me, when I realized that a fourth set of tracks was alternating with the others. These tracks would have been easy to miss; they were of small, padded feet, not hooves, much smaller than the other tracks I followed. How long they'd been slipping past me I couldn't guess, and I wasn't about to backtrack this time to see when they'd joined the trail. Seeing them was occasion enough to climb down for a close look; unless there were small wild dogs, or large foxes, running loose in Coyote's Ground, these were coyote tracks, padding happily along at the tail of the procession, mixed in with the others but never obliterated by them. Thank god they were tracks of a four-legged coyote; one walking along on his hind legs might have ended my hunt right there. Billy White Bull would say that didn't necessarily prove anything, either, since Coyote was apt to run on all fours if he was in a hurry, then stand up for a slow, dignified approach when he got where he was going.

But what was a coyote doing on the trail? They were curious beasts; maybe this one was just following along to see what all these things were, especially the buffalo, since no coyote up here could have scented a buffalo in nearly a hundred years now, and this one wouldn't have any idea what his nose was trying to tell him. But what kind of menagerie did I have out there in front of me? An old, mangy, broken-down buffalo probably too stringy to eat anyway, the hide long since past prime, and for that matter probably too old to serve Sven as a stud either; following that, a crazy artist dressed up like an old-time Indian, who should probably have been dressed like an old-time Metis instead; next a two-wheeled Red River half-breed cart, driven by someone I hoped wouldn't be wearing the wide-brimmed, flat-crowned Metis hat, bright sash around his waist, shirt and pants of embroidered deer-skin, beaded moccasins on his feet, someone I especially hoped I hadn't seen before when I was a kid, with a face I hoped wouldn't be lined and etched as though by run-off from a hundred years' worth of rain; and finally, a coyote, on four legs for now, but maybe able to get up on two when it came time to approach the camp where Charley Many Rivers and Bill Rivers would be skinning and butchering the buffalo, wrapping meat in pieces of the hide and loading the cart for their trip to wherever, trying to ignore Coyote's laments and pleas for a little food for a starving person.

Maybe, I thought, I could get there in time to prevent the slaughter, and so keep them from being in a single place at once, and then maybe whatever might happen when they all got together wouldn't happen after all. I could try; I got back up on the horse, started down the trail as fast as I could move and still be sure there was a trail.

And where the hell was Sam with that airplane? I could still hear his motor from time to time, pick up his attempts to talk to Fisher over the radio, and some of Fisher's attempts to answer back, but they were south, and keeping south, far off the trail and moving farther away all the time. Once more Sam flew over close enough to have seen me, and I pulled up, stood in the stirrups, waving a jacket at him, trying to get the dumb sonofabitch to look my way; but it was no use, and after he passed I set out again. I thought then, too late, of my rifle; a few shots fired into the air might have gotten his attention, though even those he might not have heard over his old wreck of a motor. A couple of bullets in his wings might have woke the old bastard up, if I didn't hit the gas tanks by mistake and blow him out of the sky. What the hell had ever made me think Sam was good at this kind of thing? I was out in the open, though the country was chopped and cut up, and I should have stuck out like a Bureau man at a Sun Dance.

There wasn't time to curse Sam properly; when I saw

him again, I'd do the job right, and he'd know he'd been cursed. Just then I needed to catch up to Charley and the menagerie with him. I spurred my horse on at a lope, watching the wheel tracks when I could see them flashing by, hoping the cart wouldn't turn off. Every half-mile or so I'd slow up and take a close look at the trail for a few feet, just to be certain they were all — buffalo, horseman, horse-drawn cart, and coyote — still ahead of me. They weren't far ahead now; I passed fresh coyote dung, then fresh horse-droppings, though from which horse I couldn't tell. The buffalo would, I hoped, still be some distance beyond Charley and his tired horse — the prints that horse left were walking still, and the others walked also when they replaced Charley's and one another's. I was making up ground quickly.

And I was growing more and more afraid. The old people say we won't find the missing Bundle until the world is ready to be made right again, until the buffalo come back. I couldn't believe this was the time, and yet I'd found the Bundle, could direct Billy White Bull or any of the old people to it, and I was tracking a buffalo. I also had before me a wild Indian, the wildest Metis of all, and a coyote that might — though nothing I'd seen yet said so — be THE Coyote. And to make the time complete, I wore Levis, boots, cowboy hat, carried a .38 automatic and two-way radio. Time was suspended, or was circular again — Billy White Bull would say circular as it always had been, though I'd not been able to see. After spending my life listening to the old tales and pitying myself for living when they had all ended, I found, or seemed to find, myself in the midst of one, and it perhaps the most important of all.

I didn't want to be there, didn't want it any more than had any of the old-time people who found themselves in stories with Coyote, or Wolf, or Sun, or Rolling Head, or Voracious Woman, or any of the other beings of our legends. No more, probably, had Bill Rivers wanted to be Louis Riel during the rebellion, or be Bill Rivers who shaped his ranch differently from everyone else on our reservation, who had to try to hold the ground even when it couldn't be done, and who now found himself riding the seat of a Red River cart once more, chasing again after a buffalo, perhaps as surprised to find himself there as I was. Maybe even Coyote didn't like being who he was, found himself as frightened as any, yet couldn't resist, couldn't stop being himself any more than, now, I could.

Because I couldn't stop either. Whatever was happening or about to happen, I couldn't go back, couldn't ride out of the rough country to where Sam could understand my radio again, claim sunstroke so bad I had to come in while I still could, become what I'd been before, laugh at Billy White Bull's tales I more than half wanted to believe. None of that was even barely possible. And Coyote's eyes were giving me trouble.

Once Coyote saw a bird singing on a branch, "Eyes, I want to see; eyes, I want to see," and the bird's eyes would float up and away, and when they came back, the bird saw everything they had seen in their flying. Coyote begged and cried until the bird agreed to show him how to do this thing — but be careful, it warned, never do the trick more than four times in a day. Coyote, overjoyed with his new power, promised he'd never use it a fifth time any day, and wandered off, laughing about how easy it had been to persuade the bird.

Soon he decided to try his eyes: maybe the bird had lied to him about how it could be done. "Eyes, I want to see; eyes, I want to see," he called out, and his eyes floated up and away, and when they came back, he saw everything they'd seen from above. After a while he decided to try again; maybe the bird had lied, and it would only work once. So again he called out: "Eyes, I want to see; eyes, I want to see," and again the trick worked, but this time he was a little disappointed, because his eyes hadn't seen much they hadn't seen the first time. Later he tried it a third time, and then a fourth, but then, just after he'd already used up all four tries, Coyote realized he was thirsty, and he wanted to use his new power to look for a stream or lake where he could drink. That bird probably lied to me — he probably does this all the time, and just wanted to keep me from being as good as he is, Coyote thought, and he said again, "Eyes, I want to see; eyes, I want to see," and this time his eyes floated up and away and didn't come back.

Coyote waited a long while, weeping and pitying himself, before he gave up and wandered on, blind as when he was a little naked pup with his eyes still shut — though that didn't sound right, because he didn't think he'd ever been a little naked pup; he thought he'd just walked up one day and said hello to Wolf, and ever since he'd been around. But I hadn't tried the trick at all, that day or ever, and I couldn't get Sam to notice me and let me know what was going on up ahead, so I called out, "Eyes, I want to see; eyes, I want to see," just in case it might work. My eyes had been steadily losing the clearness they'd had all morning, and the darkness around the edges was coming back, now of all times, in a way that meant the attack hadn't really been over at all, but had just given me a few hours off before it started again.

Coyote had walked blind for a while after he lost his eyes, bumping into trees, stumbling over branches and rocks, hurting himself on everything he came across, before he'd fallen on a mouse, trapping it under his hollow belly. Mouse, he'd said, I'll let you go if you give me one of your eyes. The mouse hadn't wanted to, until Coyote said he was so hungry he might as well eat it, and then it gave Coyote an eye — but not its best eye. Coyote put the eye into his socket and made his way along, still crying and feeling sorry for himself, until he came upon an old buffalo. Then he stopped and began to beg the buffalo for an eye; the buffalo was old, he said, it wouldn't need its eyes much longer, and anyway everyone knew that one buffalo eye was as good as two of most eyes — which was just one of Coyote's lies, because everyone knows buffalo can scent things much better than they can see. But this old buffalo knew all about Coyote, and knew he'd stay there crying for weeks, so he gave up an eye. This eye was worse than the mouse's; it was old, and milky, and everything looked grey and dim through it, and Coyote really couldn't see very much out of that eye either. Neither of his new eyes stayed in place very well, so he had to be careful not to lose them too, and the mouse's eye still saw everything very large, and the buffalo's eye saw very small, besides seeing through a haze, and Coyote kept getting headaches trying to make his new eyes work together. From then on he never saw very well again.

I was seeing with Coyote's last pair of eyes now; things were shifting shape and size, and my right eye was getting dimmer and dimmer. I could still hear well, or thought I could, anyway, compared to how my eyes were working. The sun was hot; I needed some shade, but this time there wasn't any nearby, just some brush down in the coulees, and I'd have to leave the trail to reach that. Before long it would be dark; I'd spent the day, somehow, on this trail, and I knew I was getting closer. If I could keep up until dark, I'd be close enough to catch up in the morning, even if the attack had its way all night.

Whether I actually saw any of the things that seemed to be in front of me then or not, I don't know, though I was sure I saw them at the time. I seemed, finally, to see that coyote I'd been following — it was big, for a coyote, and pretty scraggly looking. The hair on its hind legs had been singed, and once when it looked over its shoulder at me, I saw that its eyes weren't the same: one was so small I wasn't really certain it was even there, and the other bulged out, too large, far too large, for the socket. The shoulder it looked over was scarred with old wounds, smooth scars a knife would make, not claw marks, and I could see other lumps and scars and bruises over its body and head. The tales hadn't mentioned that; they'd always presented Coyote as though he were fresh and new each time, with none of the damage from the last tale carried over into the next, but this Coyote carried all the scars of his adventures. I was surprised he could even move.

And he was acting the fool, just as Coyote would; when the Holy Bundle had been found and the world was about to be made new again, Coyote was running along behind the cart, yapping at its wheels, then running forward to dart in from the side and nip at the horse's heels, never getting close enough to be kicked — Coyote had learned about horses somewhere, even though they weren't in the world in the old days. The old man on the cart seat drove furiously, trying to get away from Coyote, turning to cut at him with the whip and missing only narrowly each time as Coyote capered out of the way, laughing. For a couple of old fellows, they did pretty good.

As the old man turned again to slash the whip down around the cart wheels, I saw clearly — or as clearly as I could see then — whose face he wore, grim, set, unsmiling — unsmiling now, of course, trying to keep the cart from upsetting, the horse from bolting madly, but unsmiling in a way that said it had never smiled — and knew, reaching back nearly thirty years, that this was Bill Rivers, changed little since the one time I'd seen him. If any part of Rivers knew that another part of him was Coyote, he should have been yelling it out, telling Coyote to leave his relatives alone, but he was silent, and of course Coyote can't be expected to remember anything.

I couldn't see the buffalo or Charley Many Rivers through the shifting, shape-changing haze; they must have been still some ways ahead, if Rivers' cart had been able to stay on the trail with Coyote chasing it that way. From horseback I couldn't tell, so I got down, crept along on all fours with my eyes as close to the ground as I could get, reading the sign carefully as its shifting would allow. Yes, there were still one set of tracks, sometimes of a horse staying within the cart tracks, other times no cart but a horse rambling a bit from side to side on the trail, its prints often obliterated by the Coyote tracks. I still had the right trail.

But I was losing my sight, losing everything. It was time to stop for the night, sleep here on the trail, endure the sun for a while yet to make certain I'd be on the trail come morning. I was already off the horse; I had only to unsaddle, remove the bridle, slip on a hackamore in its place so I could tie the animal — letting it roam hobbled with Coyote around would be foolish; I'd want it nearby, where I could perhaps hear anything that happened — then roll out the sleeping bag and lie down to wait things out.

I could hear a roaring, and for a moment couldn't place it before I realized it was the airplane. Faintly, through the growing static in my radio, I could hear Sam: "Bird One calling Mobile One! Snook, is that you? Where the hell have you been, man? We've been looking for you since yesterday!" I looked up, saw the airplane circling overhead, coming closer and moving further away as Coyote's eyes played games with it, and I pulled the shirt off my back, waved it to let Sam know I was on the trail. He came around twice, then wagged his wings on the third circle. I could hear him over the radio, trying to contact Fisher through the static, but Fisher didn't answer. Then he flew off to the south, and I seemed to see him still, circling there, blinking his running lights and coming back my way to show Fisher the direction, then wagging his wings as Fisher changed direction and started toward me. I hoped Fisher wasn't close enough to reach me before dark, that he'd have to camp and come along in the morning. Sam came back over, circled once as he saw me laying out a camp, then headed back to guide Fisher to me. My radio was getting worse, or I was no longer able to pick words out of the static as well, but I seemed to hear bits of Sam's report to the base station back at the Agency: ". . . found him . . . won't need a search party . . . signaling he's on the trail . . . Fisher coming over . . . ways away still . . . camping and waiting there . . . going east now to see if I can . . . must have turned back north. . . " and then, a little later, as I was slipping away inside myself again, ". . . can't see anything . . . Snook says he's got the trail, though . . . will look until dark."

As I fell down into myself, it seemed obvious that Sam wouldn't be able to see Coyote or Rivers in the cart, might not even be able to see Charley and the buffalo; he hadn't seen the Bundle, hadn't touched it as I had. Whether I would still see anything the next day didn't bother me; I'd seen it once, and that was enough.

I was past caring about anything but the sun, beating on me as I lay in the open, no protection anywhere to be found. Soon it would set, and in the twilight Sam would head for his home field; but for now, the rays coasted along the earth until they found me, burned into my head, followed me down into myself. I wanted darkness, quickly, before Fisher came up.

V

Carving a Buffalo

I AWOKE TWICE during the night, first when the attack
passed off enough for pain to bring me up for a few minutes. My vision had come back, enough for the fire burning
nearby to hurt when I looked that way, not understanding
where it had come from. Around me was full dark, and I
couldn't see anything in the surrounding land after looking
into the fire. But I had glimpsed someone sitting on the fire's
far side, seeming to watch me. That it was a man I was fairly
certain, but whether Fisher who might have come up to me
in the twilight or someone else, I couldn't tell.

The second time I woke, brought up by the early morning cold, the fire had burned down to coals. The fire maker
had lain it nicely, three logs pushed end-first in, so the fire
would burn slowly away from the center, leave a bed of coals
for breakfast's cooking. That was Fisher's way of building a
fire, but any good plainsman builds a fire that way. I stood
and shook out the sleeping bag — I'd fallen asleep on top of
it, and inside was where I wanted to be just then — and saw
my companion stretched out on the fire's far side, rolled up
himself in a bag. The man stuck his head up then, asked,

"You okay, Snook?"

It was Fisher, right enough. I wasn't sure I could speak clearly yet, but gave it a try anyway. "Yeah, I'm fine. Just got cold and thought I'd better get inside this thing. Had a touch of sun, and had to lie down. You find those tracks I was following?" I didn't know whether to hope he'd found them, which would support my story that I'd been following them all along, or that he hadn't, or at least hadn't found them all.

Fisher didn't answer for a moment; he was watching me closely. Maybe I hadn't spoken as clearly as I'd hoped. "That sun can get rough out here, all right. Thought that might have been your trouble — you were pretty feverish when I came up. There's coffee in the pot there, should still be hot enough to drink. You want something to eat? Didn't look like you'd fixed anything last night."

I looked over at the coffee pot, balanced where Fisher had placed two rocks at right angles on the fire's edge. Anything hot would have sounded good, coffee especially, but I mostly wanted to hear about the trail. "I'll wait for breakfast 'fore I eat. You get here in time to take a look at those tracks?" I was looking around for my gear as I spoke.

"Cup's on the other side of the pot there, on the ground. Got it out, thought you might wake up cold, sleeping out like that. Pretty dark to see much when I came up on you; wouldn't have found you tonight at all if your horse hadn't made a fuss. Had to use the flashlight. Wasn't too hard, though — your bag was damn near right on top of the trail." He was sitting up now. "You found them, all right. Looks like buffalo tracks, and one shod horse coming along behind. Don't think they're too far ahead, either. Probably catch them tomorrow, with a little luck."

I nodded, trying to sip the hot coffee without burning myself. Lips a little numb still, so I was careful; I wouldn't feel the burn until I tried to swallow the stuff, could hurt for a couple of days that way. "Sam see them after I put him on the trail?"

Fisher reached out for his cup. "That looks good — pour me one? Thanks. Sam went over east of here after he signaled me up this way. Didn't see them, but there's brush and scrub timber enough over there to keep them out of sight, and the light was going. He'll be back this morning, I reckon, and maybe do us some good. He sure as hell hasn't seen anything the last two days — didn't see you at all. How'd you come across the trail? And where the hell you been? I lost everything not far from where I left you yesterday, and then I just drifted south, figuring that damn big buffalo'd keep going that way."

I was testing my eyes, moving my right arm, shifting my leg around a little to see if it was okay. The eyes were working, near as I could tell in the camplight, and the arm seemed fine, but the leg was a little weak, I thought. "I played a hunch when I lost the trail, probably the same place you did. Took a sashay north to see if the buffalo'd headed back for the creeks and shade, and picked him up there again. Thunder Boy get back okay?"

"Yeah, Sam got Skunk down to Charley's place before we showed up. Thunder's gonna be sick for a while, I'm betting, but they probably got him up to the hospital by early afternoon."

If Thunder Boy had gone with Skunk, he couldn't have been driving that wagon; I'd still half hoped he had, hoped what I'd seen last night was just my eyes playing tricks. Skunk wouldn't let him out until they got to the hospital, and then he'd have him under arrest, so the hospital would turn him over when he was well enough. Thunder Boy wasn't smart enough to have thought up everything he'd told us about Charley, anyway, or to have remembered it if Charley thought it up, sent him back to pick up a wagon somewhere. Though if there was a Red River cart anywhere around, I guess Bill Rivers' grandson would have known. Wouldn't have put it past Rivers to have kept one hidden down here to use in moving some of MacDonald's butchered beef.

"Mostly my fault you didn't find that trail again. I didn't leave any sign I'd gone that way — thought my tracks would be clear. Then when I came across the trail, I was afraid of losing it if I came back. I thought Sam would find me, but we were down in the coulees most of the time, and maybe he just wasn't looking north anymore. After I got up on the flats again last night, he went by south a couple of times before he picked me up. Guess it all worked out, though it was slow tracking. Might have caught up to them by now if I'd had your eyes instead of mine yesterday."

Words were coming hard, and I was speaking slowly, but seemed to be making sense; Fisher didn't look puzzled any longer. He hadn't mentioned the wagon tracks, or the coyote's, either; maybe he'd missed them in the dark. We were both half asleep — the coffee warmed us, but in the early dark morning, coffee won't wake you up much — and I wondered if he had forgotten those tracks. Anyway, I wanted to try my story out when he wasn't completely awake; anything he didn't buy I'd have changed by morning, claim he must not have heard me right, half-asleep that way. But I wanted to find out if he had seen coyote and wagon tracks, so I stuck my neck out a little.

"You see any signs of that coyote's been playing around?"

This time he did look puzzled. "Coyote? No, I haven't seen any coyotes the whole time."

"Huh. There's one been fooling around — looked like he followed the trail for a while back there. Thought he might have come in close after dark — you know how coyotes are; always up to something."

Now Fisher's a close-mouthed man, most of the time, but that reminded him of a story. "Don't I know it. There's one lives up the hills behind my old man's place, comes down maybe once a week to plague the dog. Old man says that coyote comes down by the haystacks out back, sits there and yaps until the dog takes out after him, and then runs that dog

138

all over the hills until the poor mutt can hardly walk. The old man goes out ever' now and then and takes a shot, but he misses by twenty feet every time."

"Your old man's a lot better shot than that."

"Yeah — I think he gets a kick out of it, just shoots so the dog will keep trying to run that coyote off. Damn thing never bothers the stock anyway, far as the old man can tell; lots of rabbits and prairie dogs up there in the hills. Just likes to plague that dog, and my old man sits back, laughing his ass off. Probably that coyote of yours was trying to figure out what that buffalo was — bet he hasn't ever smelled one before in his life. Maybe we'll get a shot at him tomorrow."

"Maybe." Coyote was likely to be enough trouble without someone taking a shot at him. "Well, reckon we better get some sleep. This coffee's just the thing on a cold night — thanks."

Fisher nodded, rolled himself up again, probably dropped right off. Wish I could sleep that way — never have, not even before I took this job, started these attacks, thinking I was almost hearing things all night long. Anyway, I could crawl in where it'd be warmer and try.

Fisher hadn't seen the coyote tracks, hadn't seen the wagon tracks. Or maybe he'd missed the coyote, seen the wagon tracks, and didn't figure they could have anything to do with us. Well, he'd see them in the morning, and sooner or later he'd see what was making them. What he'd have to say if we caught up and found Coyote, Bill Rivers, and Charley all quarelling over the buffalo, I didn't want to guess. But Fisher was Indian; he might find his way to understand. Sam wouldn't have a prayer. I hoped they'd stay down in the brush, and we could take them out of his sight, decide what to do next — if Coyote and Rivers together could be taken.

It had been hard work talking clearly, listening carefully enough to understand, and I was getting pretty woozy again. I needed sleep, needed to let the cool night air work on my head a couple of hours longer.

Sleep came more easily than usual, though for a while I lay there half expecting Coyote's sharp yap, his "Is there any food for a starving traveler?" or the creak of Rivers' cart with the old man himself, unbending as ever, on that hard seat. Nothing came, of course, except the ordinary night sounds; but this time there was no sense that if I really *needed* to hear something behind those sounds, I would be prevented. And that was something to think about, something to go to sleep to, even more than the thought of that damnfool Coyote, running old man Fisher's dog all over the hills, yapping and barking, while the old man sat and laughed at the dog, at that Coyote, playing the fool, yelping and snapping at Rivers' cart, making a mess out of everything, and that dog thinking he'd someday catch up, end the whole thing with one quick snap on Coyote's neck.

Next morning I had my usual hang-over, head aching, eyes seeing too clearly in the bright sun. In town, with stabs of light darting from every bit of chrome that drove by, I'd have had problems; out here, where any sudden reflection was from unmoving rock or water, I was better off.

While Fisher cooked up some bacon and eggs, I walked back along the trail. Fisher said I'd slept almost on the tracks, and he'd been right; but the tracks themselves weren't right. There were no marks of cart or Coyote, just those of a buffalo followed some distance back by one shod horse. I walked as much as a hundred yards, crossing back and forth across the trail in case the marks I remembered were off to one side or the other, but found nothing. Then I returned, went past Fisher the same distance, and still saw no change. That would make things easier for me in one way, since I'd have to offer no explanations of tracks that weren't there, and Fisher seemed to have bought enough of my story to let me get by. But it made things more difficult in my mind; I was no longer certain what, if anything, I'd seen the day before. And if all that — the tracks, the glimpse I'd had of Coyote and Rivers —

was uncertain, perhaps everything else I'd seen was uncertain also. Perhaps I'd spent the day in a haze, imagining everything: Holy Bundle, Coyote, Bill Rivers, even the cave. Only Charley's and the buffalo's tracks, unchanged since we'd first found them back on the edge of Coyote's Ground, were still there.

We ate quickly, without speaking much, then saddled up and started on the trail, Fisher once more leading. Sam came over before we'd gone far, circled once, and went off to the east. The buffalo seemed to have made no move south toward the river. The country was rough again, gullied and brushy; most of the time we could see only a few feet in any direction.

The radios were beginning to clear up; soon we'd be able to understand Sam again, and he'd be able to understand us — though that was less sure: his radio was far more powerful than our battery-powered portables. I no longer knew whether I'd heard him through the static the night before: perhaps I'd imagined what he'd be saying to the operator back at the station.

Billy White Bull would have told me that if I had found the missing Medicine Bundle we should have been on the verge of a new world, a world transformed, the buffalo about to come back. Yet the only buffalo around was out there ahead of me somewhere; or perhaps by now wasn't anywhere except as carcass, a bloody hulk to be carved into steaks and roasts by the old hunting knife Charley'd carried off from the Museum. Even if I could reach the buffalo in time to save it, the old bull was unlikely to service the cows Sven planned to buy, and there would be no herd anyway.

I was beginning to admit that the buffalo part of the legend was less likely to come true than was the finding of the Holy Bundle, unless Coyote planned to do something, or was going to do something without planning it. There's a story that once Coyote was starving — again; Coyote seems never to have been satisfied — and came across a buffalo, and asked it to help him. The buffalo, who knew Coyote would stay all day, begging and whining, said all right, he would, and told Coyote not to be afraid, whatever happened. Coyote said that was all right, everyone knew of Coyote's bravery, and of how much it took to scare him. The buffalo lowered his head then and ran at Coyote, but Coyote stepped aside at the last moment. Then the buffalo scolded him, told him not to flinch this time, and ran at Coyote again and tossed him with his horns, high into the air. Coyote rolled over and over, thinking that this was fun but might not keep being fun when he hit the ground, and managed to come down on all fours. Only when he touched the ground, he wasn't Coyote anymore, but a buffalo — not a very attractive buffalo, maybe, just a little mangy and sly-looking, but still a buffalo. And the other buffalo, the one that tossed him, said Coyote could live on the rich, lush grass which grew all around them, but he shouldn't tell anyone else the trick, or something would happen. Coyote said he wouldn't, and started to graze, marveling at how good the grass tasted, now that he was a buffalo.

That other buffalo wandered off somewhere, probably to get away from Coyote, and before long another coyote came along — an ordinary coyote, but still a relative. This second coyote was hungry, too, and stopped to envy the buffalo he saw eating grass there. But the buffalo didn't look quite right, and so he came closer for a better look, because coyotes are always curious. When he got a look at the buffalo's face, and saw Coyote's eyes glancing craftily back at him, he knew who it really was, and began to beg Coyote to show him how to turn into a buffalo.

Coyote was really hungry this time, and not just pretending, and for a while he couldn't answer because he was too busy grazing. But after a while he got tired of hearing the other coyote beg, and he began to want to show off a little, too, as he always does. So he said all right, he'd show the trick, and then the other coyote should be quiet, and let Coyote eat, because he hadn't eaten in weeks, he didn't think, though being Coyote he could never be certain about just when something had happened, or even if it had happened.

Then Coyote told the second coyote to stand fast, and ran at him. The second coyote held his ground — almost everyone is braver than Coyote — and Coyote tossed him up in the air, high. But this coyote just came down on his back, still a coyote, and got up limping and cursing at Coyote for playing a trick on him. Coyote himself wasn't saying much, because when he'd tossed the second coyote up into the air, which was what the buffalo had warned him not to do, he'd turned back into himself, and now the grass in his stomach wasn't agreeing with him; he was vomiting it up all over the place. Soon his poor stomach was empty again, and the other coyote had kicked him once or twice and trotted off, and Coyote had to go on alone, howling with hunger when he wasn't whimpering and pitying himself, and limping a little now, too.

We'd heard nothing more from Sam's radio, though we could hear his engine occasionally as he worked back and forth up ahead. Fisher was handling the tracking, and I was just following along, remembering occasionally to check the trail to see if there were any tracks besides those of Charley and the buffalo, but mostly occupied with my thoughts, and more confused by the moment.

Maybe Billy White Bull was right, and we had been getting new Coyote tales because Coyote was back, and that was also why we'd been getting new Bill Rivers tales. Perhaps there would be yet one more: about the time Coyote turned himself into a woman and a buffalo all at once, to mate with Sven's old bull and give us a crop of buffalo calves here in Coyote's Ground. Buffalo usually have one calf, sometimes twins; but surely Coyote would have twins or more, and surely if he had twins, one would be male and the other female, so as to start things over again. Or maybe both would be female, and Coyote would turn himself then into a bull buffalo to enjoy both his buffalo daughters. Maybe that was why Coyote was following along on the trail, even though

Coyote himself probably didn't know it; maybe that was why he'd tried to drive Rivers away, barking and yapping at his horse's heels, because certainly Rivers had brought that cart along to haul the buffalo meat and hide away, and Charley would probably do whatever Rivers told him, out of habit if nothing else. Surely, even if Coyote understood what was going on, Charley didn't — maybe he had Coyote's mad part only, maybe Rivers had Coyote's stubborn part only; maybe Coyote had kept, this time, and just for now, only the part of himself that could create, that sometimes understood, that had gone out and killed off monsters so people and animals could live more safely in the world. Or maybe somebody else had divided Coyote up that way for now, so that things could work out.

It was even possible that Coyote, who always liked a little love-making, planned to turn himself into a young bull, challenge the old one, or allow Rivers and Charley to have the old one, then let himself as the young bull be driven back up to Sven's place where he'd have the young buffalo cows Sven was looking for all to himself. Sven was a cheap old bastard, but he might just wind up with the kind of strong, young bull he should have bought over in Dakota in the first place, instead of saving money on an old, dried-up, worn-out animal that might not have even one more good mating.

Coyote didn't have as much to work with now as he'd had back when he'd had to carry his penis around rolled up in a box on his back, but he'd still manage to fertilize as many cows as Sven could pander up for him, and there'd be a lot of twins — though some of them might be Coyote-buffalo instead stead of true buffalo. That was always a danger with Coyote; his matings weren't apt to be true to whatever form he was in, or they were too apt to be true to what he really was.

Coyote had lost most of his penis one day when he'd been walking along and a chipmunk had started to tease him about carrying his penis on his back, like a fool. That had made Coyote mad, and he'd taken after the chipmunk, but the chipmunk had darted into a hollow tree, where Coyote couldn't come after him without making himself as small as the chipmunk was. The chipmunk had stayed in the tree, laughing at Coyote and insulting him until Coyote thought of sending his penis into the tree to crush the chip. But when Coyote had all but about ten inches in the tree, and was beginning to enjoy himself a little — he'd never tried a tree before — he stuck, and he couldn't push in further, or pull out again, and the chipmunk, who'd been pretty badly scared and was angry as soon as he saw he was going to be safe, started to gnaw. Coyote screamed and hollered and begged the chip to quit, but the chipmunk kept nibbling until he'd gnawed away all but the ten inches of Coyote that had remained outside the tree. Billy White Bull likes to tell that story; he says women were relieved when they heard what had happened to Coyote's penis, because before that Coyote used to sneak up on villages at night and hide in the brush, then send his penis through the camp looking for any woman who'd come outside her tent, and now he can't do it any more. And Coyote thought there was some good in it, too, for that matter, because he didn't have to carry that box around on his back any longer, and he didn't wake up in the night cold because he'd gotten hard in his sleep and his blanket was waving like a flag up above at the end of his penis.

But Coyote hadn't lost everything, and if he could keep the Bill Rivers part of Charley from killing the buffalo, or if I could catch up in time to keep Charley from killing, we still had a chance for the Bundle and the buffalo to work on the world again. If the world changed, then Bill Rivers' boundaries would be erased again, just as they had been in Canada, and Rivers, if he were aware of anything, would try to stop the magic, try to keep the boundaries, the lines that say this part of the world is mine, that say men can own bits and pieces of the land, can deny that there is or has ever been any wholeness anywhere to anything.

But even if Coyote succeeded — even if he intended to

try any such thing — the buffalo, whether this one or Coyote, would go north to spend its life behind Sven's fences, and there would be no herds in Coyote's Ground, no free and wild buffalo, and while the Bundle would change the people, the world around us wouldn't change. With Sam overhead in the airplane, broadcasting that we'd found Sven's bull, I wouldn't be able to get away with bringing back Charley and letting the buffalo go, or with keeping it down there long enough for it to mate with Coyote as a woman and a buffalo at once. And even if Coyote did change into a buffalo, he might change back too soon, and in his Coyote shape he'd abort a buffalo calf if he was carrying one. Even if I'd had the vision I'd always hoped for, it would probably come to nothing, or to less than it might have.

Because now Sam had finally spotted the buffalo, about five miles ahead of where Fisher and I plodded along. We could make out just enough of his broadcast back to the station to understand that before he came back over and signaled. We tried to answer him on our little radios, but he must not have been able to make us out, and we couldn't make out much that he was sending, either — just enough.

We moved along more rapidly now, trotting our horses, only slowing occasionally so that Fisher could make certain we were still on the trail. At those times I would look hard at the prints, more than half expecting to see cart and Coyote tracks mixed in, but never succeeding, and coming more and more to believe that I'd dreamed everything from the day before, even including the cave: maybe I'd wanted to find someplace cool and moist so badly I'd imagined I had; maybe I had nothing at all to tell Billy White Bull when I saw him again.

We'd closed in a bit; the buffalo and hunter were no more than two miles off now. We were getting to understand Sam pretty well, and he was even picking up some of what we said. The buffalo was grazing quietly along another creek, and Charley was still about a mile away from it, didn't seem

to know just where it was, only that he was getting close —
he was alternately watching the ground, tracking, then pausing to listen and look ahead. Sam buzzed him a couple of
times, but neither Charley nor the horse seemed to notice.
Probably the horse was just too tired to care, or had gotten
used to the airplane during the past few days.

Fisher and I had to stop whenever Sam called — the
radios seemed to work better when we weren't moving; I
supposed there were some loose wires again, and we'd have
to spring for an overhaul. The budget doesn't go too far out
here, so we have to keep repairing equipment other depart-
ments would toss or trade in. When we do buy replacements,
we can only afford the trade-ins; hell, even our fingerprint
equipment is old, more cumbersome than the kits they make
now. The last FBI man who came through asked Skunk if
he'd gotten it as part of his junior G-man kit — those FBI men
never are the best diplomats around, even off the Reservation.
We won't call them in on our own, though sometimes they
force themselves on us, since the Reservation is under federal
supervision. I hated to think of what an FBI man would
have done in this case — probably gotten in one of those
gun-helicopters and shot Charley and Thunder Boy out of
the saddle when he'd seen their war-paint back there on the
prairie, left the Tribe to pay for the horses and probably the
buffalo, too. An FBI man probably couldn't tell horses, men,
and buffalo apart, couldn't shoot straight enough anyway to
hit one without hitting everything.

I wanted to see what was up ahead, make any plans I
might without having to worry about Fisher, so I suggested
that we go another mile and then split up: I'd continue
slowly on the trail while he moved around to the far side in
case Charley tried to make a break or start the buffalo running again. It was good strategy, even if I'd suggested it only
so that I could get there first and alone, see what was really
going on and do what I could with it, and Fisher bought it.
He's the better woodsman, so it made sense that he should

take the longer approach, while I hung back and directed things — as much as possible, anyway. With the radios working again, Fisher and I could keep in touch, and even if we couldn't talk to each other directly, Sam could relay messages. I got Sam back then, let him know what was happening, told him to keep us posted on Charley. And if Charley got too close to the buffalo before we could get there, Sam should forget everything except moving that buffalo along somehow. By then, I might be close enough to help.

Fisher set off at an angle, moving around to the south where the going was apt to be a little less brushy. If the buffalo took out again, we wanted to run him west or north, back toward the Reservation. Where we were then, the Reservation was still north of us; a little further east and it would be behind. In that case, we might wind up having to put up with an FBI man — we'd been on BLM land since we'd left the Reservation, and that was their jurisdiction, not mine. If we got Charley back safely, and the BLM didn't hear of it until the whole thing was over, we'd be okay; but we'd had Sam up in the air for three days broadcasting what we were doing and we were overdue to run into one of their men down here inspecting, or at least flying over for a look at things, which is how they do a lot of their work out here.

If BLM found out, the stuff would hit the fan, all right. Though by the time BLM informed the regional office and they informed Washington, then Washington got through traffic to BIA and BIA decided what to do, got back down through their regional office to our Agent and he got the Council to meet and act, Charley, Fisher and I would be back on Reservation land, and the buffalo might be dead of old age. There'd be some explanations, but we'd claim to have been in "hot pursuit" — which was almost true anyway — and would probably get away with just filling out some reports and listening to some hollering. But if some fool ignored protocol and called the FBI directly, we might have a fleet of gunships hovering overhead by morning. Otherwise, the Tribe would meet and call a recess until I could get back and tell them what I was doing. They'd know already, of course, but faced with the Agent and pressure from Washington, they'd play the channels themselves, especially since Billy While Bull and the old folks would somehow be sending the message that this was a Tribal matter — Tribal in the old sense, before we were an American colony — and not to be settled by outsiders, even if part of it had happened off the Reservation. Boundaries, they would say, had no effect on Tribal matters, couldn't wash out anyone's Indian blood. The old people wouldn't listen to any arguments that Fisher and I were off our proper turf.

Those old people do know everything that happens; the moccasin telegraph works for them constantly. If I'd had a vision back in the cave, they'd know that, too, by now. In fact — I was glad Fisher wasn't with me when the thought struck, because I pulled up my horse and sat for maybe five minutes — they had probably known all along about the Bundle's location, may — not these old people, but those who were old when the Keeper first hid the Bundle — have decided together to hide it, keep it safe until the time came to bring it out again, and concocted the Museum story to keep souvenir-hunters and anthros away. In that case, I didn't know what my vision — or dream, maybe, which wouldn't be anything — might mean. I'd have to do what young men had always done, by going to one of the old people — Billy, of course — and asking him what it was all about, knowing I wasn't telling him anything new or startling, that he'd probably intended for this vision to happen from the time he'd first told me to apply for a cop's job. In a way, that relieved me: I hadn't as much responsibility for the world as I'd been afraid of having, and while the thought was a little deflating — that was my white blood, always wanting power — it came mostly as relief.

In the mean time, I had Charley to catch. Everything was falling into place: Fisher was circling around somewhere,

Sam was overhead, Charley hadn't seen the buffalo yet, the radios were working. Then I saw the second set of buffalo tracks.

It hadn't been necessary to track at all, with Sam guiding me and the buffalo not far ahead, so I just glanced at the trail occasionally out of habit, in case it had something to tell me, and I'd probably seen the two sets of buffalo tracks several times before I understood what I was seeing. Then I thought that maybe the buffalo had doubled back for some reason, covered the same ground twice; but when I got down for a closer look, I saw that the second tracks were smaller, didn't press into the ground so deeply as the bull's tracks. That meant either an almost-grown bull calf, or a cow.

There was worse to come: first my leg started giving me trouble again, the numbness returning so that I limped as I walked the trail, leading my horse on a long rein so the tracks would be clear to read. Then the tracks changed; where there should have been a complete set of the smaller buffalo's tracks, I found three good prints, with a coyote track where the fourth should have been, as though the smaller buffalo couldn't maintain itself, kept trying to turn back into Coyote.

I told myself that coyote I'd seen traces of earlier had slipped back onto the trail, following the buffaloes, and by chance had left a footprint imposed on one of the smaller buffalo's prints; the ground here was dry and hard, even the bull's prints didn't sink into the ground as deeply and clearly as earlier, and a coyote might not have left marks at all unless he stepped where the earth was already disturbed, so that was why I saw coyote tracks only where the smaller buffalo's prints should have been.

I hurried now, riding again as my leg grew weaker, leaning over the horse's neck to watch prints change, then sitting up to look ahead, listening to Sam broadcast that Charley hadn't found the buffalo yet but was getting close. I was nearly a mile away, and Sam said Fisher had not yet quite completed his circle to the far side. I wanted to call Sam, ask him if he'd seen a second buffalo, or a coyote, but he'd report a second buffalo quickly enough if he saw one, and I'd as soon he didn't look for the coyote.

There should have been cart tracks. If Coyote was here, whether as Coyote or the female buffalo we'd need if we were to have a herd in Coyote's Ground again, Rivers would be here as well. If the earth were about to change, Rivers would try to stop it.

Coyote would know that shape-changing can defend unchanging shapes only for a while; but the Rivers part of him, the Metis part, the Louis Riel part would never admit such a defeat. Charley, on the other hand, had listened to what Rivers had said about holding the land, but had never taken it in. He'd grown up with the wider boundary Rivers' presence and then his own had placed around the valley, had never needed the narrower lines Rivers drove into the ground for him.

I know more than I could have about these matters. Charley had never spoken of what Rivers had told him, much less of what he himself didn't know he believed, and Rivers had never spoken of anything to anyone except in ways he'd used to John MacDonald: these are my fences, these are my cattle, this is my brand, get out. But the knowledge was there, anyway, don't ask me how. Trouble was, I couldn't trust it: just as I couldn't fully trust the prints in the trail, or Sam's voice over the radio, or the radio itself.

If I had imagined everything in the cave, I might equally be imagining everything now, and I would have to act as though at least two realities were taking place around me at once, so that whichever turned out to be actual — or if both did — I would have done the right thing in it. If all these extra tracks and being were illusion, I'd have to act so as not to surprise Sam and Fisher; if Sam, Fisher, the airplane, the radio, were illusion, I'd have to act in ways that would settle with Coyote and Bill Rivers; and if everything was real and happening simultaneously, I'd have to satisfy them all.

I'd come up onto a rise, and could see out over the land before me. The buffalo was less than a mile off; Charley, who'd drifted a little south again, was nearly as far from it as I was, but he seemed finally to have seen the animal, and was urging his horse toward it. Overhead I could hear Sam's airplane, could hear him telling Fisher he'd better start closing in, and I thought I could see Fisher himself, doubling back toward the buffalo from the southwest. Rivers and Coyote were nowhere to be seen.

And then they were: there was a moment when everything wavered and I thought the attack was coming once more, at the worst possible time, and then I could see Rivers in that cart, whipping up the horse, trotting it over the rough ground, trying to catch up with Charley and be in at the kill, to keep the boundaries where he'd left them, keep anything from ever changing again. But Coyote—?

I looked at the buffalo again, and saw Coyote. He'd lost his buffalo shape, and was standing on his hind paws before the buffalo, yapping and mocking at it, while the old bull snorted and tossed his head. Coyote limped as he danced on his scarred and blistered legs, keeping his hands up close to his mismatched eyes, occasionally catching one as it fell out, replacing it without missing a beat of his dancing, or a word of his jeering. Even nearly a mile off I could see the red, angry scars on his arms, the bald spot a magpie had once pecked on his head (that's when he said magpies would eat only dead and stinking things, and they have ever since). My radio crackled and Sam's voice came through: "I think that buffalo's caught wind of something. He's looking pretty restless — there he goes again! No, he's stopped. I thought there for a minute he was off and running."

The bull had finally charged, hooking Coyote squarely in the belly and tossing him in the air. Coyote rolled over and over, landed on all fours, as pretty a cow buffalo as you could imagine. The old bull looked around, saw Coyote the buffalo, began to prance; but Coyote just tossed his head and moved toward the hunters; no time for fun.

I'd put the spurs to my horse, brought it down the slope running. The bull started after Coyote, but must have seen me, or Rivers, or Charley; he stopped, head lowered, confused. Our noise must have covered Fisher's; I could see him galloping from the other side.

Rivers had almost reached Charley, seemed to yell something at him; but Charley didn't answer, didn't seem to see Rivers any more than he'd seen Sam, Fisher and me in the airplane three days before. Charley was trying to get some speed out of his horse, but it was tired, its head hanging, its feet coming off the ground slowly, heavily, as it tried to break into a trot.

Coyote came out of the creek bottom where the buffalo had holed up, running hard, his head down, charging directly at Rivers, ignoring Charley. Charley didn't seem to see anything but the old bull; as nearly as I could tell, he wasn't paying any attention to Sam, to me, to Rivers, to Coyote, but was just staring straight ahead toward where the buffalo was. But Rivers' carthorse had seen Coyote, all right, and was trying to shy away from this buffalo cow suddenly charging at it, and Rivers had his hands full keeping the cart from spilling him out.

Coyote stopped his charge perhaps ten feet from Rivers, shook his head once, began to trot away north. Rivers had gotten the cart under control, pulled it to a stop as the cow buffalo moved away from him; he jumped down from the seat, pulled a rifle out from where it must have been lying on the floorboards, and lined up for a shot at Coyote, who was trotting as though he didn't have a care in the world.

I was busy trying to stay on my own horse; my right arm was almost useless, and my right leg was too weak to do much more than stay in the stirrup; I had to put all my weight on my left leg, try to grip the horse without help from the right, and I had the reins and saddle horn both in my left hand. The bull was still watching Coyote, but now it was also beginning to sniff the air suspiciously. I was a little closer to the bull than Charley was when I saw the smoke go up from Rivers' gun, saw Coyote take a few faltering steps and fall over; then Rivers was running forward, drawing a skinning knife from the sheath at his belt. Coyote let him get within a few steps, then lunged to his feet, charged, narrowly missed Rivers as the old man dove aside. Rivers landed hard, rolled away quickly as Coyote, bleeding from a shoulder and limping on three legs now, spun and charged again. Then Rivers was running back to where he'd left the rifle leaning against the cart, too certain of his marksmanship though it must have been seventy years since he'd shot at a buffalo, and Coyote was trotting north toward the hills.

My horse didn't shy when Coyote trotted in front of us, didn't seem to hear the clatter of Rivers' cart coming along after Coyote, or the sound of Rivers' French curses. I passed between Rivers and Coyote, and the old bull seemed to see me for the first time, to hesitate, uncertain whether to take after Coyote the buffalo cow or to run from me. He took a few steps, turned slightly to the south, saw Charley coming at him there, and turned toward the west, where Fisher had him cut off. Then he just stopped, lowering his head and pawing the earth.

I took a quick glance over my shoulder, saw Rivers pitching and tossing on the cart seat, bringing his rifle up for a bead on Coyote, heard his shot and saw the bullet kick up dust in front of Coyote and to the right. The carthorse couldn't gain on Coyote, but neither could Coyote, limping on three legs, pull away. My horse stumbled on a rough patch, and I nearly went off; after that, I paid attention only to staying on.

I was ahead of Charley, so I tried to slow my pace but still get to the buffalo first. Now that my horse had the wind up, it didn't much want to stop, and I had to let go of the horn, put all my weight behind my good arm to control my own animal. I brought it to a stop within a hundred feet of the buffalo, slipped down, trying to land on my good leg, pulling the rifle out of my saddle holster with my good left arm. Then I draped my right arm over the saddle, leaned against the horse's side, and started walking the animal toward Charley. He'd also come in close, and I was afraid for a moment he was going to charge right up to the old bull, try for a running bowshot from horseback like the old-timers; but he must not have been certain of his skill, because he stopped at about the same distance I had. The bull watched us both now, glancing over its shoulder from time to time in the direction Fisher was coming. I heard another shot from Rivers' rifle somewhere off behind, and then Coyote's derisive yip-yip-yip.

Charley was stalking the buffalo, stopping whenever it turned its huge head to look directly at him, trusting in the dimness of any wild animal's sight to camouflage him if he didn't move; this bull was old enough to be half-blind anyway. I could hear little but my own breathing and that of my horse, but Fisher must have made some noise coming through the brush on his side, because the buffalo suddenly turned broadside to Charley, looking into the brush off to the southeast.

Charley moved forward again, slipping an arrow out of the quiver at his back, nocking it on the bowstring, then half-drawing the bow as he crept. I was fifty feet from him now, and we were both that same distance from the buffalo. I took a few more steps, then brought the horse around broadside between us, leaned into the saddle and sighted my rifle across at Charley.

He ignored me, moved a few feet forward, then stopped, raised the bow and began to draw, to aim at the buffalo. I shouted: "Charley! Charley! I've got a gun on you!" He paused, seemed to listen for a moment to some strange sound far-off, glanced in my direction as though not certain what was over there, let the bow slacken a bit, then began to pull it taut. I tried again. "Charley! If you kill that buffalo I'll shoot!" I wanted to look behind at what had happened to

Coyote, to make certain Rivers didn't, in turn, have his rifle at my back, but I didn't dare take my eyes off Charley. I was aiming the rifle with my left hand out in front on the barrel, my right too weak to do more than loosely hold the pistol grip. I wasn't certain I could pull the trigger. I kept the rifle butt to my shoulder with the pressure of my body and right cheek holding it between me and the saddle; if I had to shoot, I could expect a broken jaw out of the deal.

Charley looked at me then, as though from a long way, without lowering the bow. "Even if you get me, Snook, I'll get him."

I looked down the rifle barrel. "I know that, Charley. If you want to bring the thing down, go ahead and let fly. How much do you need? I'm betting you can't kill it with one arrow, and I'll shoot to stop a second one. My right arm's in pretty bad shape, Charley; I can't promise just to wound you. There's no damage so far; we can take everything back, get you off pretty light. You know you can kill the buffalo if you want to; isn't that enough?"

Charley looked back at the buffalo, drew the bow tight, sighted down the arrow; I steadied the rifle as best I could. Then he looked back at me. "Guess you're right, Snook." He lowered the bow. "It's enough. You can ease off on that trigger." Fisher spoke up from a clump of chokecherries on the buffalo's far side, maybe two hundred feet from where Charley and I were. "That's good thinking, Charley, because if Snook missed you, I sure as hell wouldn't."

Charley put the arrow back in the quiver, braced the bow's bottom end against his left instep, and unstrung the bow. "I figured you'd be here someplace, Jim. Guess I'll have to wait and buy my buffalo steaks from old Sven."

I slumped against the horse, let the rifle slide out of my hands, slowly, so it wouldn't go off by accident when it hit the ground. For a moment I leaned there, breathing; then I straightened, turned to look behind me. Coyote and Rivers were nowhere in sight; then I saw Coyote come out of a coulee, saw him stumble and fall, saw Rivers' cart rattle to a halt nearby. This time Rivers didn't get down until he'd put another bullet into Coyote. Then he walked up slowly, watching carefully, bent over the body with his skinning knife shining in the late afternoon sun; and the cow buffalo lurched to her feet, charged and caught Rivers with her horns. As Rivers flew into the air, the buffalo changed back into Coyote, and I saw him for a moment only, unscarred, bushy-tailed, his own eyes back in his head; he stooped, lifted the box with his penis in it onto his back, and then there was nothing in the scene before me but brush and gullies.

I heard Charley's laugh, turned to see him walking toward me. "I suppose you've got some idea for herding this buffalo you want me to help with."

I just shook my head, kept myself from grinning back. "You're goddamned right I do. But first how about changing out of those clothes?"

Charley looked down at the buckskins he was wearing. "Guess you're right. But I look good, don't I? Should have thought to bring my camera along."

Fisher had moved to where I could see him among the chokecherries. "You fellas be a little careful over there — this buffalo's still kind of nervous."

I looked over at the bull; he was moving around some, but didn't seem inclined to run off just now, anyway. He was probably as tired as the rest of us, and Sven and his boys should have handled him enough to keep him from being too spooky around people, at least so long as they weren't creeping up on him with bows and arrows. "We'll keep away while Charley changes, Jim. You stay there in case he starts heading south again. Then we'll figure out what to do." I turned back to Charley. "Fisher should have a spare outfit that'll fit you. As soon as we get squared away here, you change. In the meantime, be careful with those clothes, damnit."

Charley wouldn't stop grinning. "Hell, Snook, they don't make 'em like this any more. Don't think you could hurt these duds with a blowtorch. Those old boys made 'em to last."

"Yeah. Well, watch it anyway." I took a step away from the horse, tried a little weight on my bad right leg. It held, seemed to be reviving a little; I could feel life returning to the fingers of my right hand. I turned back to the horse, bent to lift the rifle with my left hand, placed it in the saddle holster.

Charley was looking at my dangling right arm. "You mess yourself up back there someplace? Hell, you couldn't have pulled the trigger on me anyway, could you?"

I just grinned at him — my turn now. "Can't tell you that, Charley. Might affect your thinking next time I have to pull down on you. Should have shot you anyway, just on general principles. Fisher might yet, for making him sleep out the last couple of nights."

"Hell, he's likelier to thank me for giving him the excuse to get out here in the rough country and play scout. You got anything to eat?"

I took the radio down from the saddle horn. "Bird One, this is Mobile One. Do you read me?"

There was still a good amount of static, but Sam's answer came through well enough. "Mobile One, this is Bird. I read you okay. What's happening down there?"

"We've got Charley, and I think we've got the buffalo — he's not taking off on us yet, anyway. As soon as we get Charley into a spare set of Fisher's clothes and get a sandwich into him, we'll see if we can't start back tonight, cover some ground before it gets dark. You might radio in that we've got about all the Museum pieces back, except maybe the paint — looks like these ki-yis used that up pretty good. Tell Base to let Sven know we've got the buffalo, tell him to get out here in the morning with his truck — we'll try to come out on the highway somewhere. Tell Skunk to get down here with them, bring a squad car and an outfit with a trailer for these horses. I'll want you back in the morning to guide them, so we don't have to wait when we reach the highway. And you might even ask Base to find out from Sven if there's anything we should know about herding this buffalo. Charley seems willing to give us a hand, now he's through playing great red hunter. You got any suggestions about the best way to drive this thing out of here?"

The radio crackled a bit, then Sam's voice came through. "You boys disappointed me, Snook. I thought I was going to see the last of the Indian wars down there . . . Sure going to be a disappointment to my grandkids. Your best bet probably is to drift back a little south of the way you came. Land looks a little flatter, a little more open out there. I'll stay until you've made a good start, then head in and be back in the morning. That sound all right?"

"Good by me. Mobile One out."

I could hear Sam talking to the base station, still couldn't hear their replies. The static wasn't getting any better, and I figured that come morning we'd have to go back to signals again. Maybe Sven and the boys would bring horses, come in to meet us, give us plenty of men to chouse that buffalo around.

Charley was just standing there, looking around at the countryside as though he hadn't seen much of it lately. I felt pretty tired; he probably did too, especially if he hadn't been eating. I hadn't noticed the paint on his face until he came up close while I was on the radio. He'd sweat most of it off; there were dim traces of color here and there, nothing very clear. I told him to work around where Fisher was, keep an eye on the buffalo from there and give Fisher a chance to bring his horse in closer. Then Charley could change, get a sandwich from Fisher. "And fold those clothes up careful, you hear me?"

Charley was already off circling through the brush and may not have heard, but I didn't much care. The old clothes had been through a good deal, and a little careless folding couldn't hurt them much now. I kept an eye on him, just in

159

case he started for his own horse instead of for Fisher. At that point, I'd have shot him. I was just too tired to go on with this any longer.

I kept an eye on him after he'd taken Fisher's place, too. Fisher knew better than to leave him the rifle, but he might just decide to string that old bow after all; you never knew with Charley. Billy White Bull would have maintained that Charley still might turn himself into Coyote, go for the buffalo with his teeth.

There wasn't much left to do now but mop-up: get Charley and the buffalo back, see what the judge wanted to do about it. A couple months in jail up at the county seat might be the best thing — not across the river. Whoever Charley was, that jail across the river would give him too much incentive to go Coyote and break out, and I was a little afraid of what a Coyote-engineered jailbreak might look like.

I didn't feel as good as I might have about saving Sven's buffalo. Sure as hell there weren't going to be any wild buffalo down here in Coyote's Ground; Sven would be fixing his fences now, and pretty soon any calves he got would be old enough to slaughter. Even if what I thought I'd seen turned out to be the missing Bundle, and the old folks decided to finally come down here and bring it home, there wasn't going to be any change. I wondered how much of what I'd seen Charley had seen also. He didn't seem likely to talk, and I wasn't about to question him, put more ideas in his head. Maybe he hadn't seen anything, had been only a sobering drunk chasing a buffalo for the hell of it.

There wasn't much talk as we drove the buffalo west. Charley's faded paints stood out a little more once he was back in shirt and levis, with Fisher's tennis shoes — his spares always when he's tracking, in case he loses a boot heel or something — replacing the moccasins. We didn't have a hat for Charley, but he'd been out in the sun for days without one, and a little more wouldn't hurt him. He looked pretty good, really. You could see he'd had a lot of sun, but he wasn't all burned up the way Thunder Boy had been. Maybe drifting around among the various worlds out here had something to do with it — or maybe for a while he'd actually been like those old-timers who'd lived in the sun until it just didn't bother them anymore.

We found out quickly enough that you can't drive a buffalo the way you can a cow. Get too close, and the old bull would turn to face you, lower his head, paw the ground, take a few steps as though starting momentum for a good charge. But if you backed off a little, he'd turn again, walk away. Finally we just spread out, Fisher on the south, Charley on the north, me riding drag behind to the east, so the bull had to go west to walk away from the three of us at once. If Charley just didn't get some damnfool idea in his head like riding the buffalo home, we'd manage.

We'd ridden for a couple of hours, and I was trying to think over the country ahead, recall if there were any dead-end gullies where we could herd the bull in for the night, when I realized that Charley'd drifted back from where he should have been and had cut over to ride beside me. He was rolling himself a cigarette from Fisher's makings, which he must have swiped when he got the clothes and a sandwich he'd been able to keep down. I was wishing he'd look at least a little tired when he leaned over to me and spoke softly as though someone were around to hear him.

"I been thinkin', Snook. You know, that buffalo's really something to look at, now." He crimped his cigarette, licked it, started hunting in Fisher's clothes for a match. I pulled a book out of my pocket, handed it across.

"Keep 'em. You've given me enough trouble already this week, thinkin'. What you got in mind now?"

Charley lit up, inhaled deeply. "Been thinkin' I've carved horses a long while now. Might try carvin' some buffalo. Been watchin' this one, but I'd need to be around it a bit more 'fore I could really do much. You know, that old chute up the mountainside to my place is probably still in good enough shape to run him up — he's too big to get out places where a horse might break through." He took another puff on the cigarette, took it out of his mouth and looked at it. "Fisher smokes a pretty rank tobacco. Anyway, we ran this thing up there, we wouldn't have to drive it near so far, and Sven could just drive in there and pick it up in a week or so. You could probably talk him into it, do us both a favor. I could fatten it some on that grass of mine, make Sven happy, make some drawings or something, maybe even start carving."

I was too tired to shout, which would have probably started the buffalo running again anyway — but it was a near thing. "You think I'm gonna drive this thing up that hill, and fix that chute for you again? You been out in the sun too long, Charley. And there's no way Sven's gonna let you keep this buffalo. He'd be sure you were planning a barbeque. And I'm not so sure he wouldn't be right."

Charley looked hurt, or tried to. "Now, that's no way to talk. Old Sven probably would think like that, though. Maybe he'd let me come up to his place and look at it some. Didn't really see much of it but its tracks these past couple of days . . . Got a hunch people might like to have some of those buffalo statues. Guess I could even save up and buy a calf or two from Sven when he gets going." He took another puff, looked at the cigarette. "Fisher's gonna have to buy some better stuff if he's gonna keep my business, I'll tell you."

I turned in my saddle to stare at Charley. It took me a minute to get anything out. "You might make enough to pay the fine you're gonna get, you mean. You got any idea how much it cost us to have Sam up there in that airplane for four days?"

Charley looked up to where Sam was just passing overhead, probably his last before he headed in. "Oh, let's see — two, maybe three statues ought to square us."

I gave him a little hell to cover up. "Yeah, and there's me, and Fisher, and Skunk working on fingerprints at the

Museum, and towing your car, and all kinds of crap you're going to have to settle for. Hell, I might ask the judge to fine you enough to pay for a couple of cells out here so I don't have to put people in that damned town jail anymore. How'd you like that?"

Charley grinned at me again. I was getting tired of that grin. "Well, best way to handle that would be to let me take my tools into the cell with me. 'Course you'd have to bring the buffalo in ever' morning so I'd have something to work from. Might be hard on your friends over in town — that jail door ain't hardly big enough. I wouldn't so much mind serving the time that way."

"Shit. You sure as hell wouldn't. You better get your tail back over there before that buffalo drifts up into the trees and we have to take a couple more days to dig him out again." Charley nodded, kicked his horse once, and left me to my thoughts.

Charley carving buffalo. Would that be enough for the Bundle to work on? I'd have a lot to talk over with Billy White Bull, I could see that. Of course, Billy would claim that one of these days Charley's Coyote blood would tell one of those statues to come to life, and then we'd have buffalo all over the place again. Wouldn't BLM have fun trying to figure out where they'd come from? Hell, maybe the Tribe could buy a couple, let them loose down here some dark night. If the old folks liked the idea, they'd get it done all right.

I was starting to feel good again when Fisher drifted over from the other side. His voice startled me; I hadn't been paying attention to anything. "Charley got something on his mind, Snook?"

I wasn't certain I wanted to answer that. But Fisher'd worked pretty hard on this thing, and deserved at least something. He'd find out soon enough, anyway — and maybe Charley had just been playing with the idea. If people started talking about it, asking when he was going to show some of his buffaloes, then he'd have to do it or take a lot of kidding.

"Charley says he's going to start carving buffalo. Says he's going to ask Sven if he can come up and look at this one some more, look at those cows when Sven gets them, too, I guess, and probably the calves, if thus bull's young enough to get any."

Fisher stared at me in turn. "Sure. He'll be lucky if Sven don't shoot him on sight. Wish he'd thought of that four days ago, maybe saved us all this trouble."

It was good to see someone else reacting to Charley for a change. "You never know. Charley might offer to carve Sven a buffalo on the gate-post or something. I wouldn't bet he don't talk Sven into it." If Charley carved a couple of buffalo for Sven, the old boy might just drop charges against him; and he could probably work out the same kind of deal with Elwood about the horses. Then if the Tribe kept the Museum from pressing, we could get Charley off on probation, maybe make buffalo carving a condition. This thing might work out after all.

Fisher was silent for a moment. "You got any tobacco with you? I lost my fixin's somewhere."

"Got some ready-mades here — pretty old, though. Pall Malls, I think. Charley's got yours.

"Might have known. Pall Malls'll do." I held out the pack, passed over my last matchbook, made sure I got it back when he'd lit up. Fisher was still watching Charley. "You suppose that was what all this was for? Crazy bastard didn't feel like he could make a buffalo until he'd hunted one? Goddam artists, anyway."

"Could be." I'd lit up a cigarette myself. Smoke does taste good when you've about finished something. "Hard to tell with Charley."

Fisher was quiet for a time. "My old man's got one of his horses. Nice job, too. Never cared much about it myself — got my own horses out in the pasture. Bet he carves a mean buffalo, though. Maybe I'll get me one."

The buffalo'd started to drift south, now that no one

was riding on that side, and Fisher rode up alongside until the bull turned west. Then he dropped back again. He had something on his mind, all right. Finally he came out with it. "You know, Snook, I had a feeling back there a couple of times that something was going on and I was just plain missing it. You know the feeling? Like there's something just over there someplace that you should be able to see, and you can't? You ever feel that, Snook?"

It was my turn to stare at Fisher. I wouldn't have believed he'd ever been aware of anything that wasn't right in front of him to be tracked down. And I remembered something myself. "Used to have that feeling all the time, Jim. Had it when we started out on this."

Fisher shook his head, actually looked as though he was thinking. "Well, I sure been feeling it." Then, a little later: "You got any idea what any of this is about, Snook?" He wasn't looking at me, was actually looking away, as though he didn't want to admit he'd asked.

I didn't even bother to shake my head any more. "Jim, I'm not sure if I do or don't."

He pushed his horse up even with the buffalo then, far enough off not to provoke it any, left me riding drag. Another couple of hours and we'd have to hole up for the night. In the morning Sam would guide us out to where Sven and Skunk would be waiting with trailers and a squad car to take Charley off. Then things should be getting back to normal. I just wasn't sure which normal they'd be getting back to. I'd have to see Billy White Bull; I sure would.